Trust

Thea Larson

KuraCatboys
2014

Text copyright © 2014 by Thea Larson
All rights reserved. No part of this book may be reproduced or transmitted in any form or by any means, electronic or mechanical, including photocopying, recording, or by any information storage and retrieval system without written permission from the publisher. For information, address the publisher at kura.catboys@gmail.com.

First U.S. Paperback Edition 2014

Printed in the United States of America
ISBN 9780692251645

https://www.facebook.com/AuthorTheaLarson

Acknowledgements

It's been a long road getting here and I couldn't have done it without tons of help. To that end, I want to express my thanks to those that supported me in this endeavor.

First, I'd like to thank my mother, JT Larson. She helped me through emotional pitfalls that preceded the writing of this novel. I couldn't have succeeded without her support. Another reason to thank her is the lovely cover art she provided. She worked hard on it and she deserves more than thanks.

The late Janrae Frank was a wonderful inspiration for me. The aforementioned emotional pitfalls devastated me and I feared I would never write again. She gave me the confidence to write again and encouraged me to explore my original worlds. Without her, it's safe to say that this novel wouldn't be here. She left us too soon but she will never be forgotten.

I'd also like to give thanks to Ali Aftreth, Steven Beeho, and Elaine Daniels. When I was with Daverana, they tolerated my incessant babbling and helped this book to be what it is. They were great friends during the good and bad times. Daverana will forever be in my heart, as well as those who worked there.

My fiancé has been quite tolerant of me working on getting Trust published, and so he deserves a world of thanks. Love you, dear.

Lastly, I would like to thank Sara, Andrea, and everyone on my facebook friends list. They've listened intently to every whim and plot I've come up with. Thanks for tolerating me, guys.

Chapter 1

Ba-fwump.

The sound of the airlock opening echoed through the corridor that Risa Magee stood in. She barely noticed the vibration that accompanied the sound, her attention focused on the tablet in her hand. Her colleagues were in another part of the ship, ejecting things out of the airlock. What they were doing had no bearing on her current task, so she paid them no mind.

Ba-fwump.

Risa was a five foot three inch bundle of goodwill. Some said that she tied her pale brown hair back high on her head to give her a few extra inches. Such a hairstyle did a very good job of keeping errant strands out of her dark brown eyes. Her face was heart-shaped and tanned, and her frame was delicate enough to have her mistaken for a child more than once. She wore the white coat of her profession over the simple black slacks and jacket of her uniform.

Ba-fwump.

Risa made a few final notes on her tablet and turned to her next task. "This spaceship is too small for this," she sighed as she swiped her keycard at the door. "Monsters! Who would have thought?"

Ba-fwump.

The next room was as dark as the ones before it. She could hear heavy breathing and growls. Just the sound of it sent her nerves on edge. She switched on her flashlight and stepped into the room in search of a light switch. She shrieked when a creature leaped into the beam and a pair of jaws snapped shut inches from her face. Falling on her ass was the only thing that saved her from being mauled by the creature she couldn't see.

"Careful!" Risa berated herself. She tried to ignore the sounds coming from the room. She carefully played the flashlight through the door. The beam illuminated the creature that tried to take her head off. It looked like a grotesque cross between a boar and a man, with sabre teeth thrown in for good measure. Its face was purely animal, save for the grey human eyes staring at her with malice. Its front paws were all boar. As Risa looked it over, though, she saw that the fur started fading after the butt. Its calves and feet were human. The light reflected from a metal object around the creature's throat. As she watched it, it prowled towards her, only to be stopped short.

The room was wide enough for Risa to stand on the opposite side, well away from snapping teeth. After she swept the flashlight around to make sure that she was safe, she tapped her tablet to bring the screen to life.

"I found another hybrid subject," she recited as she wrote. "Mostly animal, very few human features. I am attaching a photo of the subject. It is very hostile. My recommendation is to destroy it."

She lifted the tablet so she could snap a picture. It was hard to see even with the flashlight fully on it and, annoyed, she swept the light along the walls in search of the light switch. It would be just her luck for it to be right next to the monster.

It wasn't. Risa breathed a sigh of relief when she spotted the light switch near her and flipped it on.

"Wow, this is big," she said, taking in the large room that had been revealed. It was more like a long corridor with no door at the end, and all along the wall there were creatures. They were chained up and glaring at her. As she watched a few leaped at her. They were stopped by the collars around their necks that were attached to chains secured into the wall. As she took in the sight, she noted that the further into the room she looked, the fewer moving bodies she saw.

Risa snapped the picture of the boar creature and moved on to the next creature. This one was little more than shreds of flesh and bone. When she peered closely she saw marks on the bones, as if they had been chewed on. "Next subject is dead," she noted, taking another picture. "It appears to have been killed by the creatures next to it for food." She turned off the mic and shook her head. "Of course, that's how they stayed alive. The madman in charge of this place died a week ago."

She advanced down the room like this. It was her job on this mission: document the results of Andrew Darryl's research. Supposedly, the man was a geneticist who was on the government payroll because of his work on curing diseases. After a few months without contacting his sponsors, Risa and her colleagues had been dispatched to see what was up.

None of them had expected the menagerie that greeted them. Risa had already documented two other rooms full of creatures such as this. It was very clear by that point that dear old Dr. Darryl was in fact in the illegal business of gene splicing.

Risa paused. There had been no sound for a while from the other part of the ship. "I guess they're finished with that room," she muttered. She was almost done in here, anyway.

She took the last few steps to the end of the room and found... nothing. She paused, taking in the sight. The chain in the wall disappeared behind the dead, rotting creature in the next spot over. The smell of decay was overpowering.

"I'm going to regret this," Risa sighed. She walked next to the carcass and poked it with her foot. She jumped back when a form leaped up from behind the large body.

What she saw wasn't expected. This last creature was almost fully human. She could almost mistake it for a young boy, maybe twelve years old, if not for the large, blue, clearly feline ears on his head and a long blue tail that twisted in the air behind him. They stared at each other in shock – Risa wasn't sure who was more surprised: her or the boy.

"You have blue hair," was the first thing out of her mouth. Risa backed up until she was flat against the wall. The boy seemed surprised by her words. He stood and wandered back to crouch in his spot. As he moved Risa was able to get a better look at him. He was wearing the tattered remains of a pair of shorts, and his arms and feet were covered in blood both fresh and dried. His complexion was pale, as if he'd never seen the sun. When they locked eyes, Risa saw that the dark blue irises held slitted pupils.

"I wonder if your eyes shine when the light hits them?" she wondered.

The boy didn't react. Risa inched away from the wall and crouched just out of where she hoped the chain could reach. The boy stiffened, his mouth opening to reveal large fangs. Risa flinched back from the very-feline hiss that emerged from his mouth.

The woman scrambled for her tablet. "Last subject is mostly human," she said, her voice soft so it didn't startle the boy again. "He has feline features and feline mannerisms but so far has only reacted to my actions. I'm not recommending his immediate disposal, but caution is in order."

She snapped a picture of the boy. As there was no flash there was nothing to startle him. "All right," she said, setting her tablet on the floor. "Let's see if you're dangerous."

The boy watched her closely as she inched closer and held out a hand. "Come on," Risa coaxed him. "I won't hurt you if you don't hurt me."

After a moment the boy uncurled. His footfalls were silent as he crossed the few feet and stood in front of her. Risa rose from her crouch with her hand still outstretched. This close she could see the blood around his lips. "You got hungry, huh?" she asked him.

The boy leaned forward and sniffed her hand, just like any cat. Then he reached with his hand and touched her fingertips. His fingers were cold, shockingly so. Risa let him stroke her hand interestedly, watching his ears move. They were lively, twisting and twitching in time with his fingers. She barely noticed the red streaks that his motions were leaving on her skin.

The boy clasped her hand in both of his, his expression relaxing into a smile. He looked at her and purred. "So you like me, huh?" Risa said. She smiled back and put her other hand on their joined ones. "I wonder if you were kidnapped and changed into this, or if he grew your human half. You're so young! If there was anything left of you that was human I could help you."

The boy stepped closer and leaned his head against her shoulder. It was only then that Risa realized that they were nearly the same height. "You're short," she giggled.

The boy laughed as well, then shivered. Risa freed a hand and patted his shoulder, shocked at how cold he was. Cold extremities were one thing, but he was dangerously close to hypothermia. She shrugged out of her lab coat, the boy jumping back and watching her warily. He backed up a step when she held it up.

"I won't hurt you," she said softly. She held the fabric out to him and waited for him to touch it. He left more red streaks on the material when he lifted it to his nose and sniffed it. "See? It's just a coat. Can I put it on you?"

The boy stepped back to her. Risa slowly eased the fabric over his shoulders. He tensed up, but his ears didn't go back. "It's okay," she soothed. She waited until he grasped the fabric before letting go. "It's okay. You need to get warm."

The boy seemed to realize that Risa was trying to help him and pulled the fabric tighter around his shoulders. He looked at her and smiled again.

Risa smiled back and reached for the tablet again. "After interacting with the subject, I have determined that he is not dangerous. My recommendation is to study him to learn Dr. Darryl's methods."

The boy looked with interest at the tablet. He reached for it, but Risa held it close to her. "Sorry," she apologized. "I can't let you play with this."

The boy pouted, a very human reaction that made Risa laugh. "Come on," she said, grasping the chain around his throat. "Let's see how to get you out of this."

As soon as Risa touched the metal the boy's ears went back and he growled. She snatched her hand away warily. "I won't hurt you," she soothed. "I can't get you out of here and warm if I can't get that chain off."

The boy clutched the collar, ears still back.

Risa sighed. "All right, plan B." She walked to the wall and picked up the chain. It wasn't particularly heavy, and she pulled on it experimentally. It was secured firmly into the wall and didn't even creak when she pulled with all her weight.

"I'll have to call someone to help," Risa said, turning back to the boy. As she did she saw one of her colleagues sneaking up on them, pistol raised. She grabbed the boy and pulled him behind her. "Evan!" she scolded. "What are you doing?"

"He was going to attack you!" the marine exclaimed. "I was protecting you." At six foot five, Evan Greden towered over Risa. He had short blond hair and his hazel eyes were hard as they looked at the boy. The boy growled low in his throat as he clutched Risa's arm.

"He's perfectly docile," Risa countered. "You just scared him." She patted the boy's hand soothingly. "The ones down there you can get rid of, but this one isn't dangerous."

Evan reluctantly lowered his pistol. "He may look human but he's not," he said coldly. "You know what's going to have to happen."

Risa knew full well. "'Humans are humans'," she quoted. "But this is different. It's not his fault."

The boy's grip on Risa's arm tightened. She turned to see that his ears were back and his tail was curled up. She put an arm around him protectively.

"We'll see," Evan said. "The captain will decide."

Risa watched Evan go to the entrance. The boy started at the sound of the pistol firing as Evan dispatched the other experiments. Risa winced at it as well. "Brute," she muttered. She rubbed the boy's back, then released him and stepped back to the chain.

The boy grabbed her hand to stop her. When Risa turned back to him, he tugged on the collar around his neck. "Are you going to let me try to get it off?" she asked.

The boy tugged again.

"All right," she nodded. She reached for the collar, expecting him to growl again. Instead he lifted his chin so she could see better. It wasn't a collar like she expected – the chain from the wall had been wound around his neck. It had a clasp on it, but when she tried to undo it she struggled. "Evan," she shouted down the room. "Did you manage to get any of these things undone when you ejected the others out of the airlock?"

Something clattered to the ground a few feet away. Risa saw that it was a device that looked like half a pipe. She frowned at it, turning it over in her hands. It was human tech, at least, but it wasn't anything she'd seen. "How do I use it?" she yelled at Evan.

The boy tugged her jacket to get her attention. When she turned to him, he plucked the device from her hand. Risa watched in shock as he put it to his collar and pushed the button. "So you still have some intelligence," she said, impressed.

The boy dropped the device and reached up to the collar. His fingers found the clasp and undid it. As soon as the chain slipped away, Risa jumped up. Where the metal had been, the boy's skin was rubbed raw. Fresh trickles of red made their way down his collarbone. "You're hurt," she blurted out, lifting his chin for a better look. "Come on, my equipment's in the other room."

The boy let her take hold of his hand and lead him towards the entrance. Risa skirted Evan, who was using another key device to release the now-dead creatures. She didn't like the look the marine shot at them as they approached. "Don't worry," she told the boy after they passed. "I won't let anyone hurt you okay?"

The boy looked up at her with trust in his eyes. "Hm," he agreed.

She smiled at him. "That's the first non-feline noise you made. You have a lovely voice."

Once they were out of the room, Risa collected her tools and packed the tablet away. She let the boy see her every movement as she grabbed the disinfecting laser. "This won't hurt you," she promised, turning on the red beam and pointing it at her skin. "This will just kill any germs that are in your wound."

She waited until the boy touched the beam hesitantly. Once he seemed confident that it wouldn't hurt him, he looked up at her again and smiled. He didn't move while Risa swept the beam around his neck.

While she worked, Risa was wondering how she was going to present this boy to Captain Gerald Rivers. The man was well in his fifties, far older than Risa. He was still old enough to remember humanity's first contact with aliens and the horror that ensued. It was said that his hair had gone grey from that trauma, though his hazel eyes had never been anything but kind.

She switched tools and set to healing the boy's skin. He didn't move as she worked. Even his tail was still. She couldn't help her smile as she looked her handiwork over one last time.

"I'm done," she said. She packed her tools away while the boy watched. "Now I have to convince the captain not to kill you. It will help if you're not covered in blood when you meet him."

"Eh?" the boy asked, tilting his head. His ear twitched.

Risa smiled. "Come on. Let's get you to a shower."

They made their way through the *Moreau* and towards the *Descent*, the ship Risa and her colleagues called home. Once on board, Risa steered the boy towards her quarters first. He needed to wear something more than tattered shorts, and they were about the same size. This was the first time Risa was grateful for her stature.

She grabbed her off-duty sweats and a t-shirt from her drawers. "I think this should fit," she said, turning to the boy. He was staring in interest at the picture on her nightstand. It was a holographic image of a boy. This boy looked to be about a year old, but there was an odd sort of falseness about it. Risa knew exactly why that was, but it hurt too much to think of it. Instead she touched the catboy's shoulder to attract his attention.

"The bathroom's this way," she said.

The boy straightened from his scrutiny of the picture and smiled at her. He followed obediently as Risa walked to the communal shower. When she turned on the water, though, he jumped back to the wall and hissed.

"It's all right," she soothed. She rolled up her sleeves and put her hand under the water, in part to test the temperature and in part to show the boy that the water wouldn't hurt her. "See?"

The boy didn't move from his position.

Risa sighed. "Maybe not a full shower right now then. We have to get that blood off of you somehow." She went to the closet and pulled out a washcloth. The boy watched her warily as she wet the cloth and rubbed soap into the material.

"It won't hurt you," she soothed, holding out a hand. The boy hesitated, his tail twisting with his agitation, but after a moment he lifted his hand up and put it in hers. "Good boy," she said softly. Her hands were gentle as she wiped drying blood away. He flinched at the first touch, but after realizing it didn't hurt he relaxed.

"Hee," he giggled.

Risa smiled. "You see? The water won't hurt you. It's warm, too." She guided his hand under the flowing water.

The boy snatched his hand back out and stared at it. Risa sat back and watched as he put his hand back under the water. His other hand joined it after only seconds, and then he jumped under the spray, clothes and all. He laughed in delight and let the water run all over him.

"Here," Risa said, handing him the washcloth. When he frowned at it, Risa guided it to his arms. "Wash up!" she directed. "The warm water won't last forever."

The boy seemed to understand and scrubbed his arms. When he impatiently discarded the lab coat and started to take off his shorts was when Risa turned around to give him privacy. "It seems like you have things under control," she laughed. She held up her sweatpants and scrutinized them. "Your tail won't fit through them like this." She dug in her pockets for a knife and easily opened up a slit in the material.

The first thing she had to do, she thought while she waited for the boy to finish up, was somehow convince Captain Gerald to leave the boy alive. She had no doubt that he would listen to her reasons. It was the rest of the crew that she had to deal with. It was quite likely that they would convince the Captain to slaughter this boy, just like the monsters on the *Moreau*.

Risa thought back to her near-mauling and shuddered. Those creatures were true monsters. They were mindless, ravenous beasts. This boy was so much different from them. He was intelligent, patient, and willing to trust her.

All she had to do was show the crew that the boy wasn't a monster. She just had to keep him alive long enough to get back to Earth. What would happen after that wasn't as certain, what with the government's attitude towards anything non-human, but she was determined.

The boy cried out in surprise. Risa spun around to check on him, only to find that he'd jumped from the water. He looked at her in shock, then tentatively touched the water again. He hissed as he snatched his hand back.

"The water went cold, huh?" Risa laughed. She shut it off and held out fluffy towels. "Come on, get dry. I bet you're warmer now, huh?"

His skin was no longer cold to the touch, much to her relief. She let him dry off and then handed him the clothes. He dealt with the pants easily enough, but he seemed confused by the shirt.

"Like this," Risa said. She lifted his arms up and dropped the shirt over them and his head. She tugged it down gently, paying careful attention to the cat ears on his head. She didn't want to hurt him and betray the trust he was extending to her.

The boy touched the shirt with a frown. He tugged at the hem and collar, then looked up at Risa. "I'm wearing a shirt too you know," she said, tugging at her jacket. "See?"

The boy left the garment alone. "Eh?" he asked instead.

"Now it's time to meet the Captain," Risa replied.

Chapter 2

Gerald Rivers prided himself on being a man of compassion. As the Captain of the *Descent* he knew that he couldn't always extend that compassion. When his crew disobeyed, he had to discipline them. He was the enforcer of human law when there was no one else to do so and he always thought that, when it came down to it, he could make the hard decisions.

When Dr. Magee came to his office with a non-human in tow, his first reaction was to reach for his weapon. She didn't move out of his line of sight and he frowned. "You know the law, Doctor. 'Humans are humans.' That isn't human."

"He's just a boy, Captain," Magee countered. "Darryl created him. And, as a product of Darryl's research, his ultimate fate lies with me. You know that as well as I do."

Gerald nodded. "You were given full authority over the good madman's research, I'm aware of that.

When that authority was awarded we were expecting lab specimens, research journals. I doubt the Science Board had a full-blown alien in mind."

Magee hesitated. "Captain, by this point I've spent nearly an hour with him. He's not like the monsters on the *Moreau*. He's intelligent. If you'd spend a few minutes with him you'd see that."

Gerald frowned at the figure he could hardly see. All that was visible of it was one feline ear and the tail flitting back and forth. After a moment he sighed and holstered his weapon. "All right. Bring him here." He sat at his desk and leaned forward expectantly.

Magee turned to the alien and smiled. "Come on," she coaxed, pulling on its arm. "The Captain won't hurt you."

The alien hesitated. It looked at Gerald with those inhuman blue eyes, and to the Captain's shock he saw real fear there. Then the alien retreated behind Magee with an inhuman hiss.

Magee sighed. "I'm sorry, Captain." She turned back to the creature and began to speak softly to it.

"Dr. Magee," Gerald interrupted. The woman winced and turned back to face her captain.

"He's not dangerous," Magee insisted. "He's only reacted to our actions. He hasn't made any hostile moves, only defensive ones."

"I believe you." Gerald looked down while he drummed his fingers against his desk. Humans weren't supposed to defend aliens, he lamented. Humans were supposed to think about the good of the species and eradicate any aliens that dared infiltrate human society.

He jumped a foot in the air when a hand entered his line of sight. When he looked up, he found himself staring into slitted blue eyes. The creature studied his expression for a moment, then leaned back and smiled. "Hee," it said.

Magee watched them warily. Gerald ignored her and leaned away from the creature. Now he could see it clearly. He examined the feline ears, watched the tail twisting in the air. It shrunk in on itself under the intense scrutiny, then turned and scampered back to Magee. The doctor whispered at it soothingly.

Gerald sighed. "I am ceding to your authority in this case," he said grudgingly. He wasn't sure why – the law was clear. Yet, when he stared into those inhuman eyes, he couldn't deny how human they seemed.

"Thank you, Captain," Magee said. Her voice was relieved. "Could you please send a message to the rest of the crew?"

"I will." Gerald reached for his phone, then paused. "Doctor. You know that even with my orders-"

"I understand," Magee nodded. "I am accepting full responsibility for this boy's safety."

Gerald watched them go. "He clings to her as if she were his mom," he realized when he was alone. "That's what makes him seem human."

He shook his head. He had a call that he had to make.

Risa breathed a sigh of relief when they made it back to her cabin. "I knew once the Captain met you he'd agree with me," she said as she flopped onto her bed. She looked around her cabin while the boy explored the small room. It was large enough to not technically be considered a closet, she thought. It was barely big enough for her.

Her eyes looked over her few decorations until they landed on the picture at her bedside. She reached to touch it, her fingertip tracing the holographic cheek. "You're going to need a name," she said aloud. "If you have a name, it'll help. I never thought-"

She shook her head, swallowing the lump in her throat. "I have one in mind," she whispered.

The boy padded over to the bed and looked down at her. "Hm?" he asked.

"I was going to use this name for someone else, but I don't think he'll mind if you take it," Risa said. She let her hand fall to her side on the bed. It was hard to get out. She hadn't spoken the name aloud in years.

The boy reached to her cheek. His touch was warm now as he collected the drops on her skin. Risa didn't even realize she was crying, but she wiped the tears away. The past was past, she told herself fiercely. "June," she managed to get out.

"Eh?" The boy tilted his head, studying the wetness on his hands.

"June. That's the name I'll give to you." Risa sat up and ruffled the boy's hair. "What do you think of it, June?"

"Jy-oon?" the boy repeated. He frowned as he tried again. "Joon?"

"You can talk!" Risa exclaimed, her sorrow forgotten for the moment. "Here I was thinking that you couldn't."

"Jun," June said proudly.

Risa laughed. "Almost right. Try it again. Your name is June."

The boy frowned again. After a moment he said, "June?"

"Yes!" Risa crowed. She hugged June, then leaned back and smiled at him. "One word down," she teased. "Only the rest of the English language to go."

"June," the boy repeated happily. He leaned into her shoulder and purred. Risa was taken aback for a moment, but then she smiled.

"All right, June," she said, pushing him upright. June frowned at her. "Don't look at me like that, we have a lot of work to do. The first thing we have to do is introduce you to the crew without them shooting you on sight."

June tilted his head. "Eh?"

Chapter 3

It was easier than Risa expected. She brought June to dinner with her. She ignored the glares directed her way as she led the catboy by the hand. "Everyone, this is June," she introduced. "He's a nice kid, really, just don't startle him. June, this is everyone else."

Evan rolled his eyes. "Oh great, she named it."

"Don't mind Evan, June. It's not his fault his iron's low," Risa mock-whispered to the catboy. June giggled.

"Hey! That's private medical information!" Evan yelled indignantly.

Risa ignored him. "The pretty lady next to Evan is Diane. She looks like she could break you in two but she won't, really."

Diane Ledger's glare could have cut glass. She was six-five with muscles that could put a bodybuilder to shame. If it weren't for the brown ponytail and model-good looks, she could have been mistaken for another guy. Her green eyes were hard as they shifted to the catboy.

"Just keep it away from me," she said shortly.

June clung to Risa's arm. The doctor rubbed his shoulder soothingly and pressed on. "That's Renee in the corner," she continued. "I don't have anything witty to say about him. He keeps to himself and helps keep the ship running."

"Renae?" June repeated.

"Close enough," Risa said proudly. She shot a look at Renee Tanner. The man was slight, barely topping six feet. His black hair was a bit longer than uniform-standard and his black eyes betrayed no emotion.

"Since when can it talk?" Evan asked suspiciously.

"He's human, of course he can talk. Well, when we teach him how to," Risa amended. She moved on to the next introduction. "Next to Renee we have Walter. Walter's the one that cooked this food. His meals are always awesome."

Walter Nugent was an average man. He was taller than Renee but shorter than Diane. He had no hair, but his blue eyes usually twinkled with mirth. Now, though, they were as wide as if they'd seen a snake in the room.

"And lastly, we have Gary." Risa patted June's head. "He fixes what's broken and cleans up. He does his job very well and we wouldn't have made it here without him."

Risa didn't like the look in Gary Roger's cold brown eyes. His hair was dark enough to be mistaken for black in the dark. He didn't break six foot but he still towered over Risa, and now June.

When Gary looked at June, Risa saw murder in his eyes. She vowed to stay well away from him. There was no way that she, or June, could be left alone with him and come out alive.

Risa ignored the shiver that went down her spine and tapped her chin. "Do you see anyone else, June?"

"Cap," June answered, pointing to Gerald.

"Ah, right. That's our captain, Gerald. It's not polite to just call him Gerald, so call him Captain okay?" Risa instructed. "He's in charge so you have to do what he tells you when I'm not around."

June stared blankly at her. "Jerry?" he asked.

Evan snickered.

"Enough," the Captain said. He shot a pointed look at everyone in the room before turning to Risa. "Dr. Magee, what are you doing?"

"I'm introducing June to everyone," Risa replied innocently. In reality she was gauging everyone's reaction to the boy. Most everyone seemed suspicious of June but not hostile. Gary and Diane, on the other hand, were the ones she had to watch out for. "It's time for dinner, right?"

"Only humans get to eat at the table," Diane said shortly. "People who sympathize with beasts get to eat with them."

Risa ignored the urge to glare at the other woman. She was trying to set an example for June. The catboy was behaving so far, and she thought it might be because she wasn't reacting to the hostility.

"Marine," Captain Gerald said in warning.

Diane glared back and gave no ground.

"Under the circumstances, Captain, maybe Diane's right," Risa conceded. "May I take our meals in my room?"

Walter stood and served up a plate of food. "I don't have any scraps for the animal," he said quietly.

"Then give him some food," Risa said patiently.

The cook looked at Gerald, who nodded. Walter scowled and prepared another plate.

"Thank you," Risa said. She made an effort to keep her voice light as she took the two plates. "June, get some silverware please."

The catboy looked at her, but Renee got the hint. The engineer wrapped up two sporks in napkins and held them out to June. The boy sniffed at them, then took them in his hands. "Hm?" he hummed as he looked at Renee.

"Come on, June, our food's getting cold," Risa said. The boy turned to her and smiled.

Once they were back in Risa's cabin, she let out a sigh of relief. "That went way better than I expected it to," she confessed.

June stared at the plates of food and licked his lips. He looked up at Risa hopefully.

"Of course, of course." Risa took the spork and spent the next half hour showing June how to use it. June seemed more interested in inhaling the food. Risa watched him lick his plate with a smile on her face.

Risa took the plate from the boy and stacked it with hers. Later, when June was asleep, she'd take the dishes back to the mess hall. For now, she decided to show June around the *Descent*.

"Come on," she urged June, tugging gently on his elbow. He looked longingly at the empty plate but obeyed, following her out of the cabin and into the hallway. "This is where everyone sleeps," she began, gesturing to the closed doors. "You must only go into my room, understand?"

June frowned in confusion. "Mu."

Risa sighed and tried to think of how to explain it to him. She stepped to her closed door and put June's hand on it. "Mine," she said, pointing at herself. Then she pointed at June, then the door. "Yours."

June looked back and forth, then back up at Risa. His frown lessened and his ears perked up.

Risa nodded at him, then pointed at the other doors. "Not mine," she said, shaking her head and frowning. She pointed at June. "Not yours."

June frowned again. He went to the other doors and studied each in turn, then returned to Risa's door and put his hand on it again. "June," he said.

"Yes, that's right." Risa turned his attention to the keypad next to her door. "Watch me closely."

She pushed the combination to her room slowly. She turned to June after every press to make sure the boy was watching carefully. When the last digit was pressed, her door slid open.

"Now you try," she said after the door slid shut again.

June frowned at her. Risa put his hand on her lock. "Try it," she insisted.

June's ears went back and he growled. He snatched his hand away and backed up a few steps.

Risa took in his hunched posture and his frustrated expression. "I'm sorry," she said, turning away from her door and holding out her hand. "This is all just too much, isn't it?"

June took her hand and leaned into her. He buried his face in her shirt and shook.

"I'm sorry," she repeated. "I forgot that you don't know anything. I'm trying to push you too hard." She rubbed his back soothingly until his ears came up. He looked up at her with tear-reddened eyes.

"Let's just go to bed," she decided. "It's been a long day for you."

June tagged along dutifully while she went to the communal linen closet and grabbed out an extra bedding set. He took the pillows she handed him and followed her back to her room.

Risa dumped her bundle on the floor and waited until June followed suit. Then she led June to her bed and urged him to sit down. "You'll sleep here," she said, patting him on the head. "I'll bet you've never slept in a bed before, huh?"

June just looked up at her. His whole demeanor screamed of exhaustion.

Risa lifted the blanket she hadn't bothered to pull over her bed that morning. She tapped June's legs and lifted up on the heavy cotton material of his sweats until he raised his legs and put them on the bed. She dropped the blanket, then smiled at him.

"Sleep," she urged. "I'll be here if you need me."

June caught her hand when she turned away from the bed. Risa looked back to see his anxious look, and he pulled on her hand until she turned back to him.

"What is it?" she asked.

June let go of her hand and scooted back until he hit the wall. This left enough room for Risa to sit, and so she did. "I'm not going anywhere," she assured him. "Go to sleep."

June still looked unsure, but when Risa smiled at him he returned it. He settled against the pillow, wrapped his arms around his legs, and stared up at her.

Risa tucked the blanket over his shoulders loosely and smiled. "Goodnight," she said softly.

June's face was peaceful as his eyes drifted closed. His breathing evened out almost immediately.

Risa got her bed set up and risked a quick trip to the bathroom to change into her bedclothes. When she returned, June was still sleeping peacefully.

She stood and watched him for a few minutes. What was she getting herself into? Unbidden, her eyes drifted to the photo on her nightstand. Never again, she had said when she first got that picture. Yet here she was, with a child that wasn't even human. Her first instinct should have been to let Evan or Gerald just get rid of him.

She looked at June again and shuddered. She'd seen enough dead bodies that she could easily visualize that face lifeless, his body twisted unnaturally from a limp fall. The image of those dark blue eyes glazed over and unseeing sent a wave of revulsion through her. She closed her eyes and shook her head, hard, to dispel that picture.

Even so, she couldn't deny that it was likely to happen. Humans had a visceral reaction to anything that wasn't human. She could shelter June all she wanted, but she knew that when the time came, she would have to let go of him.

She shook her head again. "Time to sleep," she said softly, opening her eyes to see that June was alive and well. She reached down to brush a few blue strands of hair from his eyes and feel the warmth from his skin. He was alive for now, and she had to take care of him. It wasn't a conscious decision, but a feeling deep in her heart. If she didn't take care of him, no one else would.

After taking the dishes to the mess hall, she climbed into her bed. She purposely positioned her bed in front of the door – if June woke up and tried to leave the room, she wanted to be awakened. It wouldn't do for him to wander out into the ship and run into Diane or Gary on his own.

It took her ages to fall asleep. Her mind drifted from June to the mounds of data it was her job to sort through. She also had to figure out how to begin doing tests on June without scaring him. Those tests involved drawing blood and seeing how his brain worked. A brain scan would tell her just how human he was. Somehow, she thought, knowing the science behind it would make it less fun.

It was with those thoughts in mind that she finally fell asleep.

Chapter 4

"All right," Risa told June the next morning. They were in her modest sickbay, just an uncomfortable chair in front of a computer monitor and a single bed. The walls were lined with cabinets that she knew were full of the equipment she would need. It was hardly large enough for her, and now she had to do her work with June in there too.

"Eh?" June asked. He settled on the bed in a cross-legged position, the best place for him to stay out of her way.

Risa reached into a cabinet and pulled out a syringe. "I have to take a blood sample," she said apologetically. June shrunk back at the sight of the needle, his eyes going wide. His ears went back and his tail puffed out.

Risa sat back and wondered how she was going to do this. "It's okay," she said softly, setting the needle aside and standing to reassure him. "It's only a prick." How could she explain it to him?

June looked up at her fearfully.

"I need this sample," she told him. She reached out a hand, the other sneaking to pick up the syringe. Sometimes with children she had to do it quickly. If she was fast enough, maybe she could get the sample without scaring him too much.

June reached for her, as he always did. She used the hand not holding the syringe to study the delicate arm he presented her, rubbing the skin in search of a good vein. It was human enough and she saw the perfect one just under his skin.

She whipped the needle around and sunk it into his arm, right on the vein. June cried out and tried to twist away, but she held on long enough to pull out the plunger with her teeth. The tube filled with red.

Risa pulled the needle out and released him with the same motion. He backed into the corner as far as he could go, looking up at her with disbelieving eyes. "I'm sorry," she apologized. She saw the red running down his elbow and dripping to the sanitary paper on the bed. She reached for him, but he growled at her.

"I'm sorry," she whispered, regretting the trick. She held both of her hands open to show that she wasn't holding anything. "I'm so sorry. I shouldn't have done that. Will you forgive me?"

[42]

Maybe it was her facial expression or maybe it was her tone of voice. Either way, June's shocked look faded and he reached for her. Risa wrapped her arms around his shoulders and spoke soothingly to him until the fur on his tail settled.

"I'm sorry," she repeated one last time. She pulled away so that she could reach into another cabinet for alcohol wipes. "This will sting a bit," she warned.

June tensed when she swiped the wet thing over the drying blood in his arm, but he didn't pull away. He whimpered when the alcohol touched the small hole in his arm, and Risa finished up as quickly as possible. She blew gently on his wet skin to help it dry, then wondered why she did it. It seemed to calm June, however, and his ears finally perked up.

She ruffled his hair and he smiled. "All right, just stay right here. It's time for me to get to work." She left June on the bed to attend to the vial of blood that this whole affair had been over.

"Time to see what you can tell me," she said to no one in particular. She slotted the vial into the computer and watched the monitor light up with new information.

"Your DNA is close to human without any of the telltale cloning markers," Risa mused, tapping her tablet with her notes. "It looks like there's only enough cat DNA in you to make your ears and tail. How did Dr. Darryl even manage to get those two to talk to each other?"

June just looked around the room, bored, while she spoke.

"Well, if you weren't cloned, you had to have been kidnapped from somewhere," Risa concluded. "I'll strip out the feline DNA and put your human DNA into the computers to search for a match."

Seeing as that would take a while, she turned to her next task. June looked at her when she turned back to him. "Lie down," she instructed, pushing gently on his shoulder. He did as he was instructed. Risa pushed a button on the bed and two metal plates slid up from the sides of the bed. June stiffened, but Risa rubbed his hand soothingly.

The scans took little time. June relaxed when the metal plates receded back into the bed. When he sat up, Risa didn't stop him. Instead, she turned her attention back to the computer so that she could look at his brain.

What she saw was interesting. "It looks like your brain is structured like a normal twelve-year-old's," she mused as she manipulated the image. "All the right places are active. You should be able to learn to talk."

June didn't react.

"Well, I'll just have to do some research," she sighed.

June sat on the bed watching as Maggie checked the vial of dark red she'd gotten from his arm. He didn't know anything about time, nor about computers. All he knew was that he was sitting there with nothing to do. It was the same as the time in the days before that, but at least this time there was no burning around his neck. He rubbed his skin, wondering at the magic that had healed him.

No heavy metal around his neck. He was used to the weight, used to trying to move and being stopped short. Having no tether felt strange and frightening. Before, he'd had a set area to move in. He knew just how far he could go, knew that nothing else that was tied beyond a certain point could hurt him.

This strange creature that had freed him was interesting. He watched her hands move over the unfamiliar device. She was similar to the man from before. Dare? Rile? He didn't know how to say that word. At that man's hands, all he had known was pain. Seeing another creature like that, June expected the same.

This woman was just so different. Dare's voice had been harsh, commanding. Hearing it made June nervous and scared. When Maggie spoke, her voice was soft. June liked it from the first time he heard it. When Maggie talked to him, she made him feel safe.

The sight of the syringe made him doubt. Maggie's trick frightened him. The fact that she seemed as upset as he, however, was what made him reach for her again. June clung to her until the shock of the trick passed, until the small dot on his arm stopped dripping red.

The wetness of the cloth she pressed against his skin shocked him. Maggie's hands were gentle as they handled his arm, each swipe of coolness taking more of the red with it. Her low tone of voice put him on edge as that cloth reached the prick on his arm. Even prepared, the sharp sting was unexpected and he couldn't help the pained sound that emerged from his throat.

The cool puff of air against the stinging was shocking even as it soothed him. He looked up at Maggie to see her soft smile. He relaxed at the sight.

June had no doubt, now, that Maggie wasn't going to hurt him like Dare did.

The woman said something, but June didn't know what it was. He looked at the device and saw some of the same images that Dare had looked at before. He didn't know what they were or what they meant, but they moved and that fascinated him.

When Maggie pushed on his shoulder, he followed the direction of the motion and settled back onto the bed. The metal plates that came up blocked Maggie from his sight. He didn't like it. He wanted to see Maggie – if he saw her expression, he would know everything was going to be all right.

He relaxed a bit when he felt a hand on his. Maggie was still there, he realized. Even though he couldn't see her, she was there. The plates wouldn't hurt him so long as she was there.

Knowing that didn't mean that he wasn't relieved when the plates receded. Maggie turned away again, leaving June to try to figure out what she was doing with that device. All he saw was brightly flashing images and trying to make sense of them gave him a headache.

He looked over at the door and sighed. Without Maggie's attention on him, there was nothing for him to do. He was, in a word, bored.

June glanced at Maggie. Her attention was focused on the moving images. He uncurled from his position and slipped from the bed. His bare feet made no sound on the cold metal of the floor and Maggie didn't look up.

He wasn't tethered anymore.

Chapter 5

Gerald looked up from his novel when he saw movement out of the corner of his eye. Midflight there wasn't much for him to do with such a small crew – his marines traded night watches, Gary had his schedule, and Renee kept to himself in the engine room. So long as they had reports ready for him at the end of the day, he didn't have to breathe down their necks.

The last he knew, Diane was in the ship's gym and Evan was holed up in his room. He could hear Walter in the kitchen. He wondered who was wandering into the mess hall at a time like this.

At the sight of the alien boy, he sighed. Magee must have some news for him, he reasoned, and he set his novel down to give her his full attention.

After a moment, he realized that June was alone. He watched the boy, fascinated, as June poked his head in the room and looked around curiously. When his eyes landed on Gerald, he tentatively stepped into the room and walked towards the captain.

"Jerry," the boy said. He stopped a few feet away and smiled at the older man.

Gerald glanced at the doorway again. Magee should have known better than to let June out of her sight. That was how she was, though. When she was caught up in her work she would ignore everything, including a bucketful of water.

June tilted his head. His tail twitched at his ankles as he studied Gerald. The captain found his eyes following that limb. If not for the ears and tail, he thought, he could almost mistake June for a normal human.

So how did he use that info?

After Magee and June had departed dinner the night before, the crew had exploded at him to protest the child's presence. "He's going to attack us in our sleep," Diane had said.

"The longer we keep him alive, the more likely it is we'll be called collaborators," Walter had grumbled.

"I don't want to go to prison for a monster," Evan had snarled.

The general consensus, Gerald decided as he and June stared at each other, was that June was somehow dangerous. He didn't know how to disprove that.

He paused in his thoughts. There was one way, much as he didn't like it. With that in mind, he stood and drew himself to his full height.

June backed up a step. His tail rose and his ears twitched backwards. "Jerry?" he asked. His voice trembled uncertainly.

Gerald hesitated.

June relaxed a bit, smiling up at him. "Hm," he said.

Gerald hated what he was about to do to this boy. There was just something about June that made the older man not see his alien features. However, Gerald reasoned, if he didn't do it then someone else would. The next person to try this would be trying to kill June.

With that in mind, he roared as he charged June, fist raised. The boy cried out and ducked the swing. Gerald swung around to see June press against the wall, his ears back and his tail twice its previous width.

That still wasn't enough evidence. Gerald charged again, hands open this time, and managed to get hold of June's shoulders. He held on tightly as the catboy squirmed under his grip. A growl echoed throughout the enclosed space, the sound vibrating up through Gerald's fingers and wrists.

June grabbed Gerald's wrists and squeezed hard. His strength was no match for an adult's. Gerald waited, but the expected claws didn't appear. Instead June opened his mouth to reveal sharp fangs and hissed.

Gerald held on, shifting his grip so that he could pin the boy with one arm. The other grabbed June's wrist. He could feel the boy's panicked heartbeat through his fingers. He yanked the limb above the catboy's head with more force than he intended. June's howl of pain made him wince.

That wince gave June an opening. Without warning, Gerald found himself on his back, fangs planted into his forearm. June straddled him and released his arm. The captain found himself staring at bloodied fangs that were mere inches from his face.

Here was the test.

Gerald deliberately relaxed. He kept his arm raised, but he let all the tension drain from his muscles. "I'm done," he said. "I won't fight anymore."

June looked at him uncertainly. His tail whipped back and forth with agitation, and his ears were flat against his skull. When Gerald didn't make a move, the boy climbed off of him and dashed out of the room.

Gerald stayed on the floor for a few extra minutes. His back was not happy with its impact against the hard metal. "I'm getting too old for this," he groaned.

Footsteps. "If I had a gun, that thing would be dead," Walter's voice said.

Gerald looked over at the cook, who looked equal parts shocked and scared. "There was no need," he said, levering himself up. He looked at the bite on his arm and sighed. "I could have handled him if he did attack after I stopped. I just wanted to see what he would do."

"Are you crazy?" Walter asked. Gerald could see the sweat dripping down his head and wondered if it was from the heat of the kitchen or nervousness. "With all due respect, Captain, you could have been killed."

Gerald shrugged. "Evan or Diane would have done the same thing. I wanted to see if June was predatory or just reacting in self-defense, as Magee said. It appears that she was right."

Magee's startled shriek echoed through the ship. "Looks like I get to go explain," Gerald said, waving his injured arm. "Please call Gary to come clean up in here."

Risa bandaged Gerald's arm while glaring at her captain. June, in her chair, shrunk in on himself and stared uncertainly at the man.

"Why did you attack him?" she demanded. Her heart was still pounding from when she first saw the blood on June's lips.

"I wasn't trying to kill him," Gerald explained. "I just wanted to see how he'd react. You were right about him, Magee. He's not violent."

"I could have told you that!" Risa exclaimed. "I spent the night with him, Captain. I fell asleep with him in the same closed room and he didn't try anything. What were you trying to do?"

"Magee," Gerald said calmly. "What if it had been Diane? Do you really think she would have stopped when he bit her?"

Risa paused. "No," she admitted. "She would throttle him for that."

Gerald nodded. "I wanted to see if June was feral. With downed prey, would he go for the kill? He didn't, and I can pass that along to the rest of the crew."

Hearing the reasons behind it didn't make Risa any happier. She looked over at June, whose ears perked up a bit as their gazes met. "It was still a horrible thing to do, Captain," she said. "But I get why you did it."

She finished tying off the bandage and stepped back to let him test it. "Why don't I get the fancy healing tools?" Gerald joked.

"I didn't want June to bolt if I brought out something he didn't like," Risa replied. She glanced at the catboy again, taking in his nervous demeanor. "I ran all of the usual tests and there aren't any bacteria or viruses in June's saliva. You're fine. Those marks should heal in a few days. If you really want the fancy healing tools, come back after lights out. When June's sleeping, I'll look at your wounds again."

Gerald waved his hand. "You're fine. It's something I deserve, anyway."

With that parting remark, he left Risa and June alone.

Risa let out a rushed breath and turned to June. "Why did you leave?" she asked. June shrunk back at her tone and she took a deep breath to calm herself. "Right, right, there wasn't anything to do and you were bored."

June just stared at her. There was still some blood on his face and Risa licked her thumb. The boy flinched when she reached for him, but all she did was rub at the red mark until it faded. She then went fishing for another alcohol wipe for her thumb.

"Come on, that's enough excitement for today," she decided. "If you're that bored, maybe you should run around."

June clutched her sleeve as she led him through the ship to the gym. Diane was there, but all she did was glare at them and continue her weightlifting. Risa ignored the heavy stare and instead walked to one of the two treadmills.

"Here, get on," she said to June. He let her guide him onto the immobile belt. She knelt down and pulled on his foot until he lifted it. She positioned it on the side of the treadmill, off of the belt, and June took the hint and put his other foot on the other side.

June watched with interest as she pressed a few buttons, then tensed as the machine came to life. "It's okay," Risa told him. She pointed downwards and waited until he looked too. "It's moving, you see? You can run on it all day if you want."

June put his hands on the treadmill's arms for balance. Risa leaned back and watched him figure out this new machine. He put a tentative foot on the treadmill, then yelped when his foot was dragged backwards. He didn't fall, but he jumped off the machine and backed away a few steps.

Risa laughed. "Watch me," she encouraged. She stepped onto the slowly-moving machine and walked at the leisurely pace. June walked up next to her, ears perked up, and stared as her feet moved back and forth across the machine. After a few minutes, Risa stepped off. "You see? It's easy."

June climbed back onto the treadmill. After a few more false starts, he finally got the hang of it. Risa watched him walk for a few minutes.

June looked up at her and smiled.

"I'm glad you figured it out," Risa told him. "Want to go faster?"

Of course there was no answer, but Risa reached for the machine anyway. She waited until June's attention turned to her before she pressed the button. The boy stumbled when the treadmill sped up, then looked up at Risa questioningly.

Risa gestured to the button. "Go on. Make it as fast as you want."

June frowned, but his ears didn't go back. Instead he turned his attention to the button. His fingers pressed it hesitantly. This time he seemed prepared for the increased speed and he started jogging.

Now that she was convinced that June could manage on his own, Risa smiled at him and wandered to one of the reclining lounges to mentally catalogue her notes for the day. She paid no attention to the sun lamp that turned on automatically above her. The warmth felt good on her face.

Chapter 6

June pushed the button to make the strange thing speed up. His legs were burning, but in a good way. He laughed in delight as he found himself sprinting as fast as he could go. How fun!

After only a short time, however, he made the thing slow down. His heart pounded in his chest and his blood thrummed in his ears. Every breath was a gasp. Even so, he felt so much better. He was full of energy, his encounter with Jerry a memory now.

The machine stopped and he flopped down to catch his breath. He looked around with interest at the rest of the room. One of the women from the night before, Dan, was looking at him with a foul expression. He didn't like that look.

Where was Maggie?

He scampered over to her and tapped on her shoulder. She looked up at him, startled, but smiled when their eyes met. She said something, but all June recognized was his name.

Her voice was gentle, however, and June immediately felt safe. He smiled at her and crouched down to be at her level. When he did, he noted the odd color of Maggie's skin. He looked up at the odd-colored light and frowned.

It was warm. June raised his hand and let the light flow over it. It was wonderful and he couldn't help his contented purr.

Maggie laughed, and he dropped his hand to look at her. She patted the thing next to her. It looked just like what she was sitting on, but there was no warm light there. June wanted to stay in this light.

Maggie patted the chair again. June stood and reluctantly went to it. When he sat down, another warm light turned on. He didn't expect it and jumped up. It only took a second for him to realize what it was and he sat down again, lifting his face to the light.

It was so warm. He purred again and stretched out so the light could reach all of him. This was something new and he loved this. The machine that let him run was fun, but this warm light was relaxing. He could stay here forever.

Risa watched as June's eyes slipped closed and noted the boy's contented smile. She thought she heard another purr from his direction. His tail drifted lazily across the floor.

June wasn't all animal, she thought as she watched him. Brain scans were one thing, but just watching him was enough to convince her of it. He was naturally curious and eager to learn new things. Last night's mishap with the door was probably because of his fatigue. When June awoke, she decided, she would try to teach him her combination again.

She heard a footstep behind her and turned to see that Diane had stopped a few feet away. "He's just like a cat," the marine observed. Risa couldn't tell what she was feeling from her voice. "Put him in a spot of sunlight and he just falls asleep, doesn't he?"

"I highly doubt that he's ever seen the sun before," Risa explained. "Look how pale he is. I'm still running tests on his blood, but I'll bet that he has a Vitamin D deficiency. He needs this sunlight."

Diane shrugged. "So are you really going to keep him around?"

Risa nodded. "Like I told the captain, he's the product of Darryl's research. This is genetic modification, but think of the applications. We could reduce health costs by tricking the human body into ignoring non-cloned tissue. A long time ago, before we came into space, the patient would have had to take immune-system suppressants for the rest of their life. Not June." She gestured to the boy, who looked up at the sound of his name. "No drugs in his system. His human body somehow thinks those ears and tail are a natural part of him and are leaving them alone."

"That's not the only reason is it?" Diane pressed. She took a seat on the floor next to Risa. "Come on, admit it. You're getting attached to him."

"Not in the way you're thinking," Risa defended. "I want to teach him to be human. It'll be a good research project."

Diane shot Risa a blank look. "So, you're telling me, after all is said and done, you'll euthanize him?"

Risa stiffened at the idea. She thought back to her musings from the night before. The idea of her own hand causing June's death sickened her and she swallowed bile.

"I thought so." Diane sighed. "Look, Magee, don't take this the wrong way."

That was a definite sign that she would. Risa listened anyway.

"You should just let me or Evan take care of it right now. You have plenty of notes for your research, so you don't need the alien anymore." Diane looked over at June's relaxed form. "You can walk out while he's like this, and when you come back in it'll be done and over with. I'll even take care of the corpse for you."

"No!" Risa cried immediately. She slid out of her seat to stand over June protectively. The catboy sat up at the sound of his name. When he saw Risa's distressed expression, he reached up and grabbed her hand. "How can you even suggest that? He's just a kid!"

"He's an alien kid. You can't keep him like a pet." Diane stood and held up her hands. "Look, it was just a thought. The longer you keep him around, the harder it's going to be on you when you have to give him up."

Risa squeezed June's hand. "When that time comes, I will." Even as she spoke those words she wasn't sure they were true. Rather than dwell on that, she turned back to the catboy. "It's okay," she said softly. "You can lie back down."

June hesitated.

"Go on," Risa encouraged. June settled back into his seat, but his ears didn't quite perk back up. When Risa sat back down, she found that June wouldn't let go of her hand.

She looked at him. His expression was worried, and when their eyes locked he squeezed her hand and smiled encouragingly. Risa couldn't help smiling back.

Chapter 7

Neither Risa nor June noticed Diane's pensive look. The marine stood and watched them for a few seconds longer than was necessary, her mouth pinched into a disapproving frown. Risa was crazy, she thought as she finally left the room. She stopped by her room to pick up a clean set of clothes.

In the shower, she tried to puzzle out Risa's motives. June was an alien, and aliens were horrid creatures that tried to force their ways on humans. If aliens were allowed to live, they would corrupt human society. That society would cease to exist.

It was common knowledge. Elementary schools taught this to children as early as possible. There was no sense in letting a child grow up thinking that aliens were okay. Anything alien had to be purged. Humans were humans.

Risa was treating this boy, this alien boy, as a human. Diane tried to figure out how she could see

June as anything more than an alien. When the marine saw him, all she could see were those grotesque ears, that creepy tail. She couldn't even bear to look into his eyes because of the slitted pupils.

All Diane wanted to do was get rid of him as quickly as possible. Her captain's orders were absolute, however. So long as Gerald ordered her to let June live, she would have to. Disobeying him was unthinkable.

However, Gerald's orders were based on Risa's judgment. The medic's judgment was obviously compromised. She was thinking of teaching the creature, for God's sake! That was just the first step. Next June would be eating with them like a human, and then the crew would see him as a human too.

Captain's orders were absolute.

Diane didn't like it. She thought it was a horrible mistake. If she had a choice, she would march right back into the gym, incapacitate Risa however she could, and then rid the ship of that menace once and for all.

She couldn't go against her captain's orders.

Diane couldn't help her frustrated sigh as she dried off and dressed. Evan walked in, his uniform in hand, and shot her a questioning look.

"What's up?" he asked as he stripped.

"Risa's treating that kid like he's not a monster," Diane complained. "I wish the Captain would let us get rid of him."

"We're all going to get in trouble because of that creature," Evan agreed. "What's going to happen when we get back to Earth and he's still alive? We're all going to be arrested and court-martialed, I just know it."

"I know I'm putting my objection on file every day. Maybe they'll spare me," Diane mused.

Her colleague paused, then nodded. "Yeah, that's a good idea. I'll do that too."

Diane waved. "Have a good night, Evan. Try to stay awake this time."

His indignant protests followed her out into the hall and she couldn't help her small grin.

Once June grew tired of sitting in the artificial sun, Risa took him back to the sickbay. This time, however, she found a tennis ball to occupy June's attention while she worked. "Why is there a tennis ball on board?" she asked as she watched June play with it.

At least it was there, and it looked like June was entertained. Risa ensured all of her cabinets were locked before turning back to the computer. The bouncing of the ball against the door was distracting, but it was better than having June walk out again without her knowing.

She tapped a few keys and brought up status windows. The DNA search results weren't back yet – not surprising, she thought, as they were still two weeks from Earth. This far away it always took a little time for communications to go back and forth. It wouldn't be until the next week that real-time communication would be possible again.

With that checked, Risa loaded up the analysis of June's blood. The basics were done, but the computer was still busily prying open all of those cells. An in-depth report on what made June's body tick would take two more days.

Still, this was enough information for a basic report. Risa cracked her fingers and opened up the form. She found herself talking out loud as she typed. It was a habit she picked up after spending so much time alone in this room.

"Preliminary analysis on June shows that, as I determined before, his human features are predominant. Blood samples indicate that he is nearly indistinguishable from humans. So far, there was one feline protein in his system that I must analyze to determine its purpose.

"June's brain scan shows normal activity. I will need to scan it again to test his responses to various stimuli. My preliminary hypothesis, however, is that those scans will return the same results.

"Over the next few days I plan to collect more data. I will do an in-depth scan of June's whole body. I am interested in seeing how his body has adapted his feline features so seamlessly. I am also wondering how deep his humanity is. I want to know he works from the inside out.

"On to the behavioral tests. Captain Gerald has tested his response to danger and June appears to prefer to flee rather than fight. In situations without a danger element, June is eager and curious. He learns new information quickly and can adapt that knowledge to new situations. Case in point: I showed June to how to speed up the treadmill, but not how to slow it down. He figured that out on his own."

Risa tapped her finger against the keyboard with a frown. Was there anything she was missing? She couldn't think of anything, and so after a quick scan for spelling errors she saved the file and emailed it to Gerald.

She glanced at the clock. She had time for her usual sickbay check before it was quitting time. June watched her as she opened the cabinets and marked off her checklist. Quite a few times Risa had to stop so June could examine something that interested him. The only time that she refused this was when it came to medicine that he could open and contaminate.

June didn't seem to mind the refusals. There was always something else that caught his eye and he handled everything carefully. When Risa got to the cabinet that held the syringes, however, June scrambled backwards with a hiss.

"It's all right," Risa soothed. She quickly counted her stock of those and closed the cabinet. As she turned to the boy she held her hands out to show they were empty. "No more tricks. I promise."

June slid off the bed and checked the desk behind Risa. Once he found that it was empty, he smiled at her and took the proffered hands. To the woman's surprise, he leaned forward and wrapped her in a gentle hug.

"June?" Risa asked cautiously.

The boy rubbed his head against her cheek and purred.

Risa hesitated before she rubbed his head between those ears. The purr intensified, and June pulled back so he could smile at her. The warmth in his eyes shocked her.

It was an expression of perfect trust.

Risa wrapped her arms around him. No, she realized, she wouldn't be able to give him up. She couldn't identify the feeling in her chest at this moment. It was glowing and warm, radiating peace to every part of her.

They stood like that for a few minutes. It was June that pulled away first. He retrieved his tennis ball and once again curled up on the bed. Risa watched him and wondered just what it was that he was thinking at that moment.

She wished he could tell her everything. She doubted that Darryl had ever shown him any kindness. The thought of June in pain made her shiver uncomfortably.

Risa had to teach him, she decided. Not just for science or research, but so that she could get to know him. He was very reactive and his emotions were easy to determine, but he couldn't really tell her anything.

Plus, he was smart. He would learn to hide his sorrow when he saw that Risa was happiest when he was. Before that happened, Risa wanted him to be able to tell her if anything was wrong.

It was with that in mind that she caught the ball as June bounced it towards the door. "Come on," she coaxed. "It's time to go."

June looked up at her and smiled. "Go," he agreed.

Chapter 8

Renee peeked out of the engine room. When he saw that there was no sign of the boy, he sighed with relief and headed for the mess hall. It also served as a common room when there were no meals to be had. Tonight, it was his duty to set up movie night.

It was Gary's turn to pick the movie, he remembered, and with that in mind he headed for the other's storage closet. They met up just as Gary was packing away his tools.

"Hey," the engineer greeted with a wave. "Got your movie?" Despite his efforts his voice remained quiet, and he inwardly scowled. He hated that he was so quiet. He envied Evan for his outgoing personality.

Gary nodded. "It's in my room, some old American classic about monsters. I figured Risa needed some reminding."

"Yeah," Renee agreed, though he really didn't feel it. He didn't understand the intense hate that the rest of the crew had for June. Sure, he was wary of the boy, but he didn't honestly believe that June could be dangerous. Word had already spread of Gerald's encounter.

Weren't monsters always able to get their mark? Cute little monster rabbits were able to down a horse in movies. Monster dogs could take down elephants. The fact that June was a child wouldn't deter him if he was really a monster. If the boy wanted them dead, he already could have killed them.

Renee wondered if June would be at movie night. Their brief interaction the night before made him curious about the boy. He wanted to interact with him more, see if he really was as dangerous as everyone claimed. At the same time, he was scared of finding out those accusations were true.

It was always the timid ones that died first, after all.

He followed Gary and collected the data drive. With that in hand, he could get movie night started. He was already mentally putting the equipment together in his head when he passed the sickbay and bumped into someone.

"Oh, sorry," he said quickly, backing up a few steps. It took him a second to realize that he'd run into June. Risa was a watchful presence behind the boy, but the child didn't seem angry. Rather, those blue eyes were staring into Renee with a burning curiosity.

The engineer swallowed hard. June's tail twitched and the boy frowned at him. Even so, those large blue cat ears didn't go back. Rather, it seemed as if June was trying to measure him.

Renee shook his head. "I'm sorry," he repeated. He leaned down to June's eye level and smiled. "I should have looked where I was going."

Hesitantly, he reached a hand out to June.

The boy studied him for a moment longer before smiling and reaching back. Renee was treated to a quick, painless squeeze before June turned back to Risa and grasped for her hand. Renee straightened and turned his attention to the medic. She was still watching him carefully.

"How is he?" he asked.

Risa pursed her lips. She pulled June back just a step, but the boy resisted. He looked at Renee with a shy smile, one that was returned. After a second, Risa relaxed.

"I'm sorry," she apologized. "Diane suggested something earlier that put me on edge. June's doing fine."

"He's a smart one," Renee agreed. His eyes drifted back to June. He was entranced by that tail, at how it flowed and weaved around the boy's legs. It was hypnotizing. He shook his head and turned his attention back to Risa. "Are you bringing him to movie night?"

Risa seemed undecided. "I doubt the rest of the crew will be happy if I do," she noted.

"June might like the movie," Renee pointed out. He hesitated. "I can sit with you if you want. As extra protection I mean. I don't know how much good I could be, but maybe it will help?"

Risa smiled at him. "Yes, that would. I appreciate your offer, Renee."

Renee smiled back. Speaking up was a good thing, he told himself. When he turned to the mess hall to get the film set up, he was still smiling.

The movie was already starting when Risa walked into the mess hall with June in tow. She had stopped by her cabin to change out of her uniform. She was more comfortable in her casual slacks and blouse.

June didn't seem to mind that he had only one set of clothes. It bothered Risa, and even as they sat down she glanced at him. This was his second day in those clothes. She had to search her wardrobe for something for him. She just didn't have much that wasn't feminine. Life on board the ship was cramped enough, and no one had room for many personal items. A few non-uniform-standard clothes, a few trinkets, those were what everyone had.

Renee smiled at them as they sat down. The table in the mess hall was shoved out of the way, all of the chairs arranged so that the large screen in the far wall was visible. They were sitting at the far end, close to the door just in case.

"Why did you have to bring that thing?" Evan's voice asked.

Risa scowled in his general direction. In the darkness, it was hard to pick out individual faces. "Why shouldn't I bring him? Just watch the damn movie, Evan."

Someone started to protest, but Gerald spoke up. "It's movie night, and Risa is of course welcome. As is anyone on board the ship. June is on board and so he's welcome. Anyone who doesn't like it can leave the room."

There were a few mutters of distaste, but those settled down as the first spaceship touched down and the alien invasion began.

June didn't like the darkness. It reminded him of the time he was locked in that room, with those creatures next to him. It made him wonder if there was a creature just out of reach. If he moved in the wrong direction, would he get attacked?

He reached next to him and found a hand. It was Maggie's hand, he could tell, and he squeezed. She was there. Nothing could get him now.

Maggie whispered something in his ear soothingly. He thought he was starting to understand one of those words. Okay. It was a good word. When Maggie said it, he felt safe.

A loud sound startled him and he jumped. His head darted around looking for the source of it, and he saw a light on the other side of the room. It was some more moving images, but these were different from the ones that Maggie and Dare looked at. They were of creatures like Maggie and Dare, but they were running.

June frowned at the screen. Those people seemed terrified of something. Then a large lizard creature came into view and lunged forward. He cried out and ducked his head, but nothing happened.

Did the lizard miss?

Cautiously, June looked back at the images. The lizard was still there, still lunging, but now it was bounding sideways across the wall. There were humans still on the screen, still running, but they were soon pounced on by the lizard.

What were those images? They looked so real, but they didn't seem to be able to hurt him. June let go of Maggie's hand and stood. He wanted to see what that thing on the wall was.

He heard speaking behind him, and his name was passed around. He looked back and saw everyone from the night before, though he couldn't remember all of their names. There was Maggie, then that man from the hallway earlier. When he looked at June, the boy could tell that he was nice.

It was Jerry and the man that he'd met after Risa. Evan? June thought that was his name. Evan was saying something loudly, but Jerry was arguing back. Their attention wasn't on him right now, though, so June turned back to the moving images.

He reached them, then shrieked as the giant lizard on the screen seemed to try and snap at him. He jumped back, heart pounding, but he saw the lizard vanish and be replaced by more screaming humans.

It was more magic, like Maggie's red light. Maggie's magic didn't hurt him, so June hesitantly reached to the picture again. When the lizard came on again, he flinched but didn't cry out again. As he thought, the lizard didn't leap from the image. It was there, but it wasn't a danger.

June touched the lizard. It was smooth and tingled a bit. When the lizard vanished and more humans showed up, they were smooth too. He traced his fingers all along the image and found that it was the same all over. No matter what was showing, it still felt the same.

It wasn't real. June blinked once he realized that, frowning. What was real? He thought back over everything that had happened, trying to catalogue it. Images weren't real. They just were. Things he could interact with, touch and smell, those were real.

He tapped on the image a few times to be sure. Nothing he did affected the images. He tapped the lizard's eyes and it still saw its prey. He shielded the humans with his hands but they were still eaten.

Nothing that happened in that image was actually occurring.

Chapter 9

Risa couldn't help her chuckle at June's antics. "He still hasn't figured out that it's just a movie," she said fondly.

"He looks like he's learning," Renee pointed out.

They stopped watching the movie and instead watched June. About halfway through the movie he seemed to understand that what was on the screen wasn't real. He returned to his seat and curled up. In the faint light of the movie, Risa could see a puzzled look on his face.

Tomorrow, she decided, she would draw up a curriculum for him. She would start to teach him words, and then maybe she could explain the concept of fiction to him.

June glanced at her. There must have been something in her expression because he smiled. "Okay," he assured her.

The word surprised Risa. June was picking up on things faster than she thought. She smiled back.

The movie ended and someone turned the lights on. Risa was already thinking of a shower and then bed.

"Hey, Risa," Evan called. The rest of the crew dispersed around her while she turned, June's hand in hers to keep him from wandering off.

"Do you want me to stay?" Renee asked in that quiet voice of his.

"We'll be okay," Risa answered. "Thanks."

Renee seemed hesitant but he waved and walked out anyway.

There was an awkward silence for a while. Evan finally sighed. "June, come here," he said.

June looked uncertainly up at Risa, then back at Evan. The marine held out a hand and gestured. Hesitantly, the boy walked over to him and took that hand.

"What are you up to?" Risa asked. Evan ignored her, studying June's hand. He traced his fingers over the smaller ones as if looking for something.

Once he was satisfied with that, he tilted June's head up so their eyes could meet. The catboy didn't react.

"He's not human," Evan said at last. He rubbed June's head between his ears and smiled a bit. "I can't deny that he acts human, though. The way he tried to protect the people in the movie from the monsters was touching, sort of, in a strange kind of way."

June seemed to enjoy the attention and purred.

"So you're not going to try to convince me to kill him?" Risa asked skeptically. This wasn't what she expected from Evan.

"I don't think you can avoid it, but I'm not going to be the one trying. I say let's give the kid a chance. Why couldn't we just chop those ears and tail off? He'd be human enough after that." Evan turned June around and pushed him gently towards Risa. The boy took the hint and returned to her side.

"Why don't you chop off your hand?" Risa replied. It was a reflexive response. Her mind was already thinking of that and wondering at the repercussions. When she looked at June, she couldn't imagine him without those features. They were a part of his character.

Evan shrugged. "Hey, I'm just trying to help."

Risa paused, glancing at June's clothes again. "Maybe you can help."

"How do you mean?" Evan wanted to know. He looked at June as well, frowning.

"Do you have anything he can wear?" Risa paused. "Well, obviously you won't have any pants," she amended, thinking of the marine's height. "Even a shirt would do. Something that he can wear that isn't this." She gestured to June's borrowed outfit.

"Ah, right. He doesn't have anything." Evan scratched his head as he thought. "Well, I guess he can have one of my t-shirts. It's long, so if anything he can sleep in it right? I'll go ask around and see if I can convince Gary or Walter to give up some boxers or pants."

"Just one extra set of clothes would be good," Risa said.

"I'll get on that right now. I have to stay up all night anyway." Evan pushed past her and out of the mess hall.

Risa wondered what was going on in Evan's head. This wasn't the reaction she'd expected from him at all. It was nice to not have to be wary of him, but at the same time she wondered at his motive.

"I don't trust him," she said after a minute's thought. "He's being way too nice."

"Hm?" June asked.

"He tried to kill you the first time he saw you. I can't believe that just this quickly he's changed his mind." Risa shook her head. "Well, if he can get you something to wear, I don't mind. Come on, it's time to take a shower and then go to bed."

When she got to her cabin she paused, remembering her thought from earlier. "June, look," she said, catching the boy's attention. June watched her fingers as they danced over her door's keypad.

Once she put the last digit in, the door slid open. June made to enter but Risa caught his arm. The boy looked up at her in confusion when the door closed.

"Now you try," Risa encouraged. She urged him forward and put his hand on the keypad. Unlike the night before, June didn't growl. He frowned as he stared at the buttons, fingers tracing them, and then hesitantly pushed the first one.

Slowly but surely he input the combination. Risa watched his expression as he did so. She had a clear view of his jubilation when he pushed the last button and the door slid open. He let the door close so he could open it again, then giggled in delight.

"I knew you could do it," she told him. This time she went into her room and started digging around in her drawers for a change of clothes.

Evan met her outside the shower with a bundle of clothes in his arms. "The Captain and Renee had some clothes they could loan. Gary and Walter looked at me like I was insane when I asked."

Risa sorted through the bundle and found a few pairs of drawstring shorts, underclothes and several shirts. One of them was long enough to reach past June's knees. "This one's yours, I'm guessing," she said when she held it up.

Evan looked a bit sheepish. "It's all I had."

"Thank you," she said. She kept out a pair of the boxers and the large shirt. The rest of the clothes she folded and put under her arm. "I'll take them to my room after we're done here."

"How are you going to take a shower? The kid's, well, a kid." Evan didn't quite glance at Risa's obvious feminine features, to his credit. "I doubt you want to corrupt him this early."

Risa laughed a bit. "Of course not. There's that one privacy shower, remember? Renee uses it all the time."

"Oh, right. I guess you've thought it all out. Have a good night, Risa, June." Evan waved and turned towards the mess hall. If Risa had to guess, he'd spend his night watching more movies on the big screen. As long as he didn't wake the whole ship up with them she had no problem with it.

After a moment's hesitation, Risa decided to put June in the privacy shower – such as it was. It was the only showerhead with a curtain around it. She could keep her eye on it to make sure the boy didn't peek at her.

In all honesty, though, she didn't think June would do something like that with lecherous intent. He was far too innocent. His attention seemed to be focused on exploring the world around him.

She tried to bury the thought that June wouldn't live long enough to lose that innocence. She could win over her crewmates, but the law was the law. June was obviously not human. Once she could no longer justify keeping him alive for her research...

Risa shook her head to dispel that thought. There was no need to think so far ahead. June was here, and now. Right now, they had to take their showers.

June learned the shower knobs easily enough. Risa closed the curtain on him and turned her attention to getting clean. It didn't take her long. June was still showering by the time she finished and dressed.

With time on her hands, Risa turned her attention to the new clothes for June. All of the shorts and boxers would need to accommodate the boy's tail. It didn't take her long to cut the requisite slits in each one.

When June emerged from the shower, Risa had the long shirt and a pair of boxers ready for him. He dried off and didn't hesitate when he was handed the clothing items. The boxers bemused him, however, and he fiddled a bit with the open front.

"I think you'll figure that out when the time comes," Risa said wryly. June laughed, then donned the shirt. It was so large that it made him seem smaller than he was.

Risa collected June's discarded clothes. "I'll just put these in with my laundry," she decided. "Now come on, June. Let's go to bed."

Evan watched Risa and June leave the bathroom and shook his head. That alien boy confused him. How could a creature so inhuman act just like a little kid?

Granted, June wasn't an ordinary kid. He was more of an infant than anything. Evan thought back to just a little while ago. June's insistence on messing with the screen ruined movie night for Walter and Gary, he knew that right away. It annoyed him, too, but then he'd really sat there and watched June.

The boy's reaction to the screen didn't mesh with Evan's definition of monster. The way he'd gone from fright, to curiosity, and then finally to acceptance was strikingly human. It reminded Evan of his younger brother. They were eight years apart and Evan remembered vividly when Tracey hit his toddler years.

Evan blinked. That was it. June reminded him of Tracey. Tracey was now off on the fringes somewhere studying those beasts that threatened humanity. Even so, it was hard to forget the sibling that made Evan so jealous.

Still, the fact that June wasn't human made him wary. Everything he'd ever been taught told him aliens weren't to be messed with. If they wouldn't run, they had to be eliminated. He remembered hearing about an altercation between a human ship and one of theirs. The aliens had attacked without warning, destroying the ship and killing everyone on board.

It was stories like that that made Evan unwilling to fully trust June. Even interacting with him didn't make it easier. Without the ears and tail, perhaps things would be different. Things got amputated all the time. June would probably forget that he ever had them soon enough.

"What about the fangs?" he asked out loud. He remembered Walter's account of the fight earlier that morning. "Well, there are enough vampire freaks out there. He'd fit right in."

Unless Risa got rid of those obvious alien features, Evan couldn't really trust June. The Captain seemed to think he was perfectly docile, though. Renee didn't even seem to care that June was an alien.

That puzzled Evan. Humans were humans, and June definitely wasn't human. The best thing would be for someone to gain Risa's trust, then dispose of the boy without her knowing. She'd find out, probably not very long after the fact. The deed would be done by then and there would be nothing she could do about it.

Still, when Evan looked at June, all he could think of was his own brother. What he'd told Risa before was the truth. When the time came to kill June, he wouldn't be the one to pull the trigger. After the fact, he would treat the boy with all due respect. He would ensure that June got a decent sendoff.

Only a few people on board seemed to be willing to actually do the deed. Diane would, of course. She was well-trained and would follow any order she was given. Gary had already offered. Walter still hated June, but he didn't seem the type to actually do anything about it.

Evan sighed and went hunting for the television remote. This wasn't something he wanted to spend his night on watch thinking about. All he wanted to do was find something he hadn't watched much before. Later he would tour the ship and listen for any alarms that might be going off.

Chapter 10

The next morning, June followed Maggie into the room where they got their food from and looked around curiously. He could see someone through the small opening into another room. His gaze fell on the table. It was covered in items that he'd never seen before.

Maggie sat him down on one side of the table and walked around to the other. June looked up at her curiously, and when their eyes met he smiled. She smiled back, then gestured towards the objects. June followed her hand as she picked up something that was brightly colored and round.

Maggie said a word and held out the object. June reached for it, but the woman frowned and held it out of reach. When he looked up at her, she said that word again.

June drew his hand back. What did Maggie want?

She held the item out and said that word again. June watched her lips and tried to figure out how to say it. That's what she wanted, right? If he said the word, she'd give him the item.

"Ah," he started to say. That wasn't right. He frowned and tried again. "App... apple?"

Maggie beamed at him and handed him the item. June studied it. "Apple," he said again. That's what this was. It was called an apple. Now what could he do with it?

Maggie said something, and when June looked up she had her hand out. He put the apple in her hand and watched as she took out a knife and sliced it up. She put one piece in her mouth and handed the rest to him.

June hesitantly bit into the apple slice. It was an awkward shape and he had to maneuver it around his fangs. The drop of juice that touched his tongue sent his eyes wide from surprise. It was delicious!

He ate the rest of the apple and licked the juice from his hands. There were no more apples on the table, to his dismay. He wished he could have another one.

Maggie said his name and he looked up at her. She picked up something else and said another word. This new object was the same as the thing he played with yesterday. It could bounce so high! If he could say that word, would Maggie let him play with it again?

Maggie repeated the word. It was short and June figured it out quickly. "Ball!" he exclaimed, holding out his hands for it. Maggie chuckled and gave him the ball. He got up and sent the ball bouncing towards the wall. When it bounced in another direction, he chased after it with a delighted laugh.

After only a little while Maggie came and got the ball again. June pouted but followed her back to the table. There were so many more objects to learn about. He wondered how much more was food. If they were as tasty as the apple, he couldn't wait to get his hands on them.

Only about a third of the objects were food. By the time everyone else filed in for the third meal of the day he could name and identify everything on the table. June looked up at Maggie, cup in hand, and saw that she was proud of him.

He scrambled to his feet and rushed to hug her, cup clattering to the floor in his wake. She was so warm and smelled nice. June buried his face in her shoulder and enjoyed the sensation of feeling safe. Maggie stroked his hair and he couldn't help his purr.

A hand tweaked his tail and he yelped. When he looked for the culprit, Evan winked at him and went on his way innocently. June couldn't believe that the man had done that. He frowned as he stared at Evan.

Risa watched June's expression as the catboy frowned at Evan. "Why'd you do that?" she asked. June stepped out of her arms and went to retrieve the fallen cup, still displeased.

After a second Risa amended that assessment. June didn't seem upset at Evan. Rather, he looked downright mischievous when he lifted the cup. He brought it back to the table and picked up the glass of water instead.

Renee helped Risa stack the items on the table into a storage container to make room for the food Walter was bringing out. When everyone sat down, June didn't. Instead, he wandered around the table while sipping from the glass until he got to Evan.

The marine yelped when June tipped a few drops of water down his neck. The catboy set the glass down and dashed out of the room with a mad cackle. All Evan could do was shake his head. The rest of the room went very still as they looked at the doorway.

The marine saw their look and glared at them. "Don't even think about it."

"You saw what he just did," Gary growled. His hand was already on a knife.

"What I saw was an innocent prank," Gerald told him. "It's just some water."

Walter, Gary, and Diane frowned and shared a look.

"I deserved it," Evan insisted. "Don't hurt him for that. I shouldn't have pulled on his tail."

The rest of the crew settled down into their seats. It was clear by their expressions that they were unhappy with their captain's decision.

"You kind of deserved that," Risa agreed, looking at Evan. June poked his head back into the room and saw that Evan was still sitting. He walked up to Risa and smiled at her.

Walter dished out the food and passed the plates around. He saved Risa and June for last. As he put the food together, he scowled.

With her and June's plates in her hand, she turned to leave. "Come on, June. Let's go eat in my room." She didn't even wait for the others to dismiss her. They'd made their feelings clear enough that first night.

It grated at her nerves, even as she smiled at June and waited until he was seated to give him his food. He picked at it, evidently not hungry. It wasn't surprising. Every food item that he named earlier she'd allowed him to eat.

Thinking of that made her wonder how many apples were on board. Even after everything else, the apples seemed to be what he enjoyed most. As she continued to teach June, she could use the apples to reward him.

Still, Risa wished that the rest of the crew would warm up to June. She was tired of having to sequester the boy away. Her feelings aside, June would learn faster if he could interact with the crew. She didn't want him to feel isolated.

Their eyes locked again and June smiled. "Okay," he insisted. "Food okay."

He was learning to string his words together. Risa returned his smile. "Yes, it is okay. It's good too."

"Good," June agreed.

Risa pushed June down so he was lying on the sickbay bed. The boy patiently stayed where he was put while Risa turned back to her computer. "It's time for that full-body scan," she said lightly. Her fingers keyed it into the system. All along the sides of the bed metal plates rose up.

"Maggie?" June called. His voice was uncertain but not scared.

"It's okay, June," Risa assured. When did the boy learn her name? It occurred to her that she never tried to teach it to him. Even so, despite the mispronunciation, June knew it. It surprised her.

She turned to the bed and leaned over so she could smile at June. "It's all right," she told him. His face relaxed almost immediately. "It will only take a few minutes. Just stay still."

His hand twitched upwards, then stilled. He closed his eyes and hummed a bit. Risa's smile turned fond and she turned back to the computer to see how much longer it would take.

Only the promised few minutes later the panels retreated. June sat up as soon as they started to retract. He reached across the few feet to Risa and clutched at her coat.

"Don't worry," Risa said, putting a hand over his. "You'll have to do that again, but it won't be as long." She just had to put together some sort of program to test June's brain while he was in the scanner. Image recognition was one possibility. Neuro science wasn't her specialty, and it would be a few days until she could do the research.

While she sorted through the data, she accidentally brought up the list of medical programs stored on the computer. She sighed and was about to go back to her data when she paused.

"These look like-" she murmured, scrolling through the programs. She tapped her tablet and locked all of the sensitive data. A few minutes later, it was prepared.

June looked up at her when he held out the tablet. "Here," she encouraged.

He hesitated, his ear twitching. When Risa didn't scold him he reached out and took the device. June looked at it with a puzzled frown, then up at Risa.

It took a little while to show June how to use the device. The touch screen responded to the lightest press of his fingers. Once he figured that out, he was quick to pick up on it. Risa left him to it once he settled back against the wall. His ears were lively as his fingers chased the pictures on the screen.

"Learning games can come in handy," Risa mused. She turned back to her computer and began studying June's body. "It looks like I was right. You're human on the inside too."

She paid close attention to June's head and tail. Human anatomy blended seamlessly into feline. "It's artistic," she mused. There was something graceful about the way Darryl had crafted June.

Risa glanced at the boy. June's face was set in concentration while his fingers jabbed at the screen. He was curled up just like countless other teens given a tablet and a lot of free time would be. If not for the ears twitching madly on his head and the tail thumping on the bed he could be a normal boy.

That brought her back to Evan's question. What if she put June under and removed his ears and tail? He was still learning about the world. It was feasible that he would only notice their loss for a short time. A year from now, two, and it was likely that he'd forget he ever had them.

Risa turned back to the screen. It was theoretically possible. She went back to the scans of his head and studied the way his human head twisted itself into the feline ears. June also had a set of human ears. As Risa studied the image intently, however, she realized that he was hearing primarily through the feline set.

She decided that a little test was in order. "June," she called. He looked away from the tablet, ears perked up. Risa went to a cabinet and pulled out a sturdy length of cloth. "It's okay," she said as she wound it around his head. June tensed when she gently flattened his ears, but he didn't move until they were securely bound.

That should muffle any sound he heard through those ears. Already Risa could see the effect. June shook his head and frowned, then reached up and rubbed at the cloth. He looked up at Risa with a confused frown on his face, his tail twitching in agitation.

"It's all right," Risa soothed. She kept her voice soft. When he didn't react to it, she raised her voice. "June, can you hear me?"

June tilted his head, then fell to his side. He seemed surprised by this and tried to stand up, but he wavered dangerously on his feet. Risa caught his shoulders before he could topple over again.

"Yes, these ears are essential," the doctor concluded. She sat June down and quickly freed his ears. She found her attention caught by them, though, and she spent a few minutes stroking them gently. They were warm, and the fur was silky smooth under her fingers. She ran a finger around the base of one to feel how the fur merged into the soft blue strands of hair that fell over his eyes.

Her fingers followed the curve of the ear up. The fur at its very tip was fine and feathery. Risa gripped the ear gently between two fingers, comparing the feel of the top and bottom. Even the bare skin under her thumb was soft.

"Maggie?" June asked. Risa realized that she was still holding his ear and snatched her hand back.

"I'm sorry, that was rude," she said. She could still feel the fur on her fingertips. It was strange. Over these few days she knew he had those features, but it was only now that she realized how real they were.

[97]

Somehow she thought that if they were touched, handled in any way, they would blow away and leave only a human June behind.

Yet, as they looked at each other, Risa realized that June could never lose those ears. It was just as she'd told Evan – she might as well cut off her own hand. It was doable, but it would leave her forever crippled. June, without his cat ears, would never be the same. He could forget the tail after some phantom limb syndrome shenanigans. His ears, though, would traumatize him forever.

June leaned forward and took her hand. Risa let him guide it back to his head and he looked up at her with a gentle smile. "Okay," he said.

Did he like when she petted his ears? She resumed her slow stroking and watched as his eyes closed. He had a contented look on his face. There was, strangely, no accompanying purr this time.

Risa could feel the soft smile on her face as she looked at June's. She felt peaceful when she saw his happy look. Without really realizing what she was doing she leaned forward and pressed a gentle kiss to his forehead. June wrapped his arms around her and put his head on her shoulder.

This wasn't anything Risa had felt before. It was warm, filling her heart from the inside until she thought it would burst. She pressed another kiss to his head and squeezed him tight. June clutched her tighter, a sigh that sounded suspiciously like her name emerging from his lips.

They stayed like that for a few moments until Risa remembered that she was supposed to be studying June. She let him go but couldn't help smoothing the hair back from his head so she could see his happy expression clearly. His smile filled her heart and she left another kiss on his forehead.

She turned back to her computer and blinked at it. What was she supposed to be doing? June's body scan stared back at her and she remembered. "Right, I have to compile my report," she said out loud. She switched to the form and stared at it. Her brain didn't want to work.

She sighed, saved the data, and closed down the computer.

Chapter 11

"Any sign of her?" Walter asked. He was seated around the mess hall table with the rest of the crew. Only Risa and June were absent from their little meeting.

Gary drummed his fingers on the table. He knew what they were going to be talking about here. It was a formality – no matter what happened here, each crewmember would act on his or her decisions. Still, he hoped that he was wrong. Pessimism was always his failing.

Evan peered down the hallway from his chair. "She just went into the gym with June. We should be okay for a while."

"Especially if June curls up under the sun lamps," Diane agreed. Gary could picture that – June was mostly human, but even humans liked to bask in the sunlight. He shook his head clear of those thoughts when she turned to Gerald. "So, Captain. Why did you call all of us here?"

Gerald stood and looked them all over. Gary wondered what was going on in his head. His captain could hide his thoughts behind a mask of professionalism. When he spoke, his voice was emotionless. "As you all know, we'll be regaining real-time communication with Earth sometime tomorrow. I know all of you have people you want to talk to, supervisors over your departments you need to check in with."

"Hell yeah," Gary muttered. He couldn't help his glance towards the door. Something told him that Risa might walk in any minute. At least he could still recognize that it was paranoia. "So you're wondering just what we're going to say."

Gerald nodded. "I understand that you all dislike having June on board. The law is the law, and if one of you receives the order to eliminate him, there will be nothing I can do. I just ask that you think, hard, before you report about June."

Gary agreed with him. He had his own reasons for keeping June quiet, but his shipmates didn't have to know that. Actually, he reflected, his crewmates couldn't know his reasons. If only he could trust them enough to actually tell them. Again, his paranoia kept him from it. If even one of them decided to take offense, everything would come crashing down.

"Why wouldn't we?" Walter snarled. "He's an alien! He's dangerous, and he's bewitched Risa into thinking him sane. We need to protect ourselves and if you won't let us-"

"I just ask that you consider the consequences of your actions." Gerald locked gazes with each member of his crew. "I'm trusting your judgments on this matter. All I'm going to tell my superiors is that we have a live specimen of Darryl's. I'm not going to elaborate any further on that. If I receive the order to eliminate June, I will carry it out. Then I will make sure that whoever causes that order spends the rest of the journey home miserable."

That order wouldn't come because of Gary. Then again, he had his own reasons. He shot aside glances at his colleagues and tried to gauge their reactions. Only Walter and Diane looked severely displeased. Gary matched their expressions.

"That's not unbiased at all," Diane muttered. "So, Captain, what do you think? Really?"

The scowl faded from Gary's face. What, indeed. His Captain didn't seem to be playing favorites with their resident alien, but neither was he specifically endorsing June. His attempts to be fair were admirable.

"Yeah," Walter asked. "What makes you so sure that this monster won't hurt us?"

Gerald frowned. "Have you really watched him? I interacted with him briefly when Magee brought him on board. He's a child in every sense of the word."

Gary agreed with that assessment. But infant predators could still be dangerous. One didn't have to look any further than Earth's own ecosystem to see that.

"Even child aliens are dangerous," Renee pointed out softly, as if reading Gary's thoughts. "Look at all the movies about it. But if June wanted to kill us, he would have by now. I don't think he's a danger to anyone here or on Earth."

Gary shook his head. Maybe Renee wasn't quite as in sync with him. At least it was essentially the same thought.

"June is innocent, completely," Evan agreed. "Risa's having to teach him everything - how to speak, how to eat, even how to use the restroom. When we get to Earth, I know people won't even bother to get to know him before killing him. While he's here, why can't we give him a good life?"

Gary wondered at that as well. Still, June wasn't human. Most would think he didn't deserve a life, much less a good one.

Diane frowned at Evan. "I thought you hated him."

Evan shrugged. "I thought I did too, but then I watched a movie with him."

"So what made you change your mind?" Gary asked him. He was honestly curious. It wouldn't affect his decision, but maybe he could understand.

"Like I said, June's an innocent. He didn't ask to be made into this. Why should we punish him for that?" Evan shook his head. "Just... talk with him. You'll figure out that he's a good kid."

"I don't trust him," Gary huffed. He knew he was all bluster. The question was, did his crewmates?

"It doesn't matter if you trust him. Avoid him if you must. Just please, let this boy get as much of a life as he can," Evan implored his crewmates.

There were a few mutters and traded glances. "Fine," Gary bit out. "Just tell Risa to keep him away from me." He'd seek June out on his own when the time was right. He just couldn't let his crewmates know, or else things would get out of hand quickly.

"Me too," Walter said darkly. "I don't want anything to do with him."

Gerald looked at Diane. "What about you?"

The woman shrugged. "To be honest, I don't care. I'm not allowed to kill him anyway. Evan takes care of contacting our department supervisors. Whatever he tells them, he tells them."

Evan smiled at Diane. "Thank you."

Gary nodded mentally. Of the whole crew, only Diane and Evan were from the same branch of service. Gerald held sway over shipboard matters, but as it concerned their respective duties, he had to concede to his and their superiors. If Diane was truly going to let Evan handle communications, maybe June stood a chance.

"Is there anything else?" the Captain asked, looking around the room. Everyone was silent. "Very well, you're all dismissed."

Everyone stood and made their way to their respective corners of the ship. Gary turned to his storage closet to make sure all of his supplies were stowed correctly. Even as his hands worked, his thoughts were on the alien creature they were harboring.

Gerald was asking the crew to take a risk. Humans who showed sympathies to aliens were harshly punished. Anyone caught harboring aliens, sentient or no, was known to vanish quietly in the night. Gary frowned as he took in the weight of that risk. He was fairly sure most of the crew could get away with the "following orders" excuse.

If things truly went to hell, Risa would take the full brunt of the blame. It was on her authority that June was on board. The few times that Gary caught sight of the two, Risa wasn't treating June like the alien he was. The doctor had small smiles on her face when June was learning. Her eyes rarely strayed from him when they were with the rest of the crew.

Gary shook his head. Getting attached to creatures was a human thing to do. Why else would humans have cats, dogs or any number of animals as pets? Risa's actions, though, weren't those of an owner training a pet. They were remarkably similar to a mother's interaction with a toddler. Risa watched mindfully while June explored his world, ready to step in only when he was in danger.

It was those actions that would lead Risa down a dark path. Gary only hoped that when June was dead, Risa would be able to manage the fallout. She was a wonderful doctor that was a credit to the military. It would be a pity to let one lapse in judgment ruin her career.

Chapter 12

The beeping of her computer startled Risa the next day. She was browsing through the files gleaned from Darryl's servers and jumped a foot when the note sounded. When she searched out the source of it, she couldn't help her cheer.

"And we have communications!"

The beep, she found out, was her long-neglected searches finally completing. Earth's many-million-large missing children's database had turned up... zero results. Risa frowned at the screen.

"Well, that was useful," she muttered. She put June's DNA back into the system, keyed in a search for everything but children, and set that to working.

An hour later, after she had found what she wanted in Darryl's notes, the search beeped again. Two results blinked at her, with a few less-than-optimal matches thrown in for flavor. She blinked, then frowned and looked over at June again.

"That can't be right," she muttered. She keyed in the search again and let it run.

June peered over her shoulder. "What is?" he asked.

Risa beamed at him. "Those games are doing wonders for you!" she said.

The boy blinked at her. "Huh?"

"Nevermind," Risa dismissed. "Go back to playing, June. After this search finishes again we'll go to the gym. You'll be able to run around as much as you want there."

June wandered back to the bed and picked up the tablet again. Risa marveled at his progress with the device. Since just yesterday he'd mastered the infant games and moved on to the toddler ones.

She turned back to her computer. There were notes to peruse. With only a week left before they got back to Earth, she had to find a way to justify June's existence.

Even with that knowledge in her head, she couldn't help sneaking glances at the boy. June was muttering to himself, repeating the words that the tablet spoke to him. The voice-recognition software was able to determine whether or not the words were right.

Risa was so fascinated by Darryl's notes that she again was surprised when the search finished. "I really need to stop doing that," she said ruefully. When she looked at the results, she frowned. They were the same as before.

According to the results, June had two direct relatives in the system. Risa pressed a few buttons and called up their public records.

"Andrew and Meredith Darryl," Risa read. "Married fourteen years ago in Idaho, United States." She frowned. "I never knew Darryl had a wife." Then she paused and looked at June in shock. "You're Darryl's son!"

June looked up at her and tilted his head, ear twitched. "Hm?" he asked. Then the tablet made an angry sound and he looked down at it, aghast. "No!"

Risa shook her head and turned back to the record. Ten years ago, she read, Darryl and his wife had been driving home one rainy night. An accident robbed him of his wife… and his son was declared brain dead.

Her jaw dropped.

The name was redacted from the reports, but by all accounts, Darryl's son's body survived the accident. The toddler's brain, however, was rendered mush. The last thing on public record was Darryl's withdrawal of the boy from professional medical care. It had been done against all medical advice. According to the reports, the doctor on duty had recommended removing the boy from life support.

"He didn't want to let his son go," Risa whispered, again looking at June. Even with the name redacted, the report was clear enough. Broken bones. Shattered internal organs. Even if he'd recovered, he would have been crippled. Organs would have had to been cloned just to get him functioning again. The costs would have been exorbitant. Yet, to a grieving father, money was but an object.

Her curiosity was stirred. June simply couldn't be the same boy in this report. Cat ears aside, there was no sign that he was anything other than a healthy child. With injuries like those listed, he should hardly have been able to walk correctly. At the same time, with her training, she could look at June and picture him with those injuries.

She could sympathize with Darryl. If she had the money, the resources, she too would do anything to get back what she'd lost. The more time she spent with June, though, the further that ache seemed. Their eyes met and he smiled at her.

He couldn't have been the boy in the report. Darryl must have discovered a new cloning technique. Risa needed more samples. If she could figure out this technique, maybe that would justify June's life.

Doing so would condemn him to a life of experimentation. He would be prodded with the needles he hated so, treated as less than the lab animals of centuries past. His time not being poked would be spent in a cage. Sure, he might get a room, and maybe a bed, but he wouldn't be allowed to leave. He would be caged just as surely as if the walls were bars.

Risa shook her head. Just so long as he lived, it would be enough to start. In time, if she worked at it, perhaps she could make life easier for him.

Maybe, once everything to be learned from him was had, he would be released. Maybe the government would allow her to take him in.

Not likely. Risa sighed and leaned back in her chair. Looking at the blank silver ceiling helped calm the sudden pounding in her head. The government's position on things like June was quite clear. Once June's usefulness was at its end, so was his life.

Risa felt the prickle of tears in her eyes and swiped at them. "Enough of that," she scolded herself. She dragged her thoughts from that to the computer in front of her. So much of Darryl's motivations were clear. The only question that remained was, why cross his son's DNA with that of a cat's?

Darryl's notes would tell her that. Tomorrow. She minimized her current task and started her computer on another. It wouldn't take long, but having it done in the morning would give her time to act on the information it would give her.

"Come on, June," she said, standing and stretching the kinks out of her back. "Let's go to the gym."

Night watch, Diane groused in between reps, was the worst.

There was nothing to do. During the day, at least, she could wander around the ship and peek in on her crewmates. Renee could usually be found with his tablet in hand, crouched in the corner watching something or other. He had a fondness for old movies of all sorts, though most of them were animated. Diane didn't see the point in it.

Gary was chatty while he cleaned, at least. Over the past week they'd shared many conversations about what to do with their unwanted guest. Most of them required distracting Risa somehow. There hadn't been a good medical emergency on board during this trip. Diane was willing to shoot herself in the foot if it meant they could be rid of that menace.

It was Evan that dissuaded them. "June will be dealt with when we get back home," he declared. "Just leave him be."

Diane scowled at the memory. Just leave him be, she repeated in her head. Just leave him be to corrupt them all.

There was a noise from the hallway and she paused. It wasn't uncommon for someone to wander around at night. Those wanderings were usually limited to bathroom breaks. On this ship, at least, there was no sneaking between cabins for late-night "meetings". Two weeks to get to Darryl's remote outpost and two weeks back. It didn't leave time for crewmates to get to know each other.

Diane smirked. She'd been on shorter voyages where crewmembers had fallen prey to their basic instincts. She had a few thoughts to that effect herself about a few of her crewmates. Alas, her dropped hints went unanswered. At least it was only six days until home. She could make due until then.

She stowed the weight away and wiped the sweat from her forehead. If she played her cards right, she might not have to wait too long. It all depended on who was in that hallway and whether they had company.

Before she could make it to the door, she paused. It wasn't a crewmate that was up and wandering about. Diane looked disbelievingly at June as the alien boy wandered into the room. He looked around through bleary eyes before yawning over to the lounging chairs.

It was only another second before he was curled up under the sun lamp, soundly asleep.

Diane stared at him. It couldn't be this easy. Yet, as she glanced to the door, there was no sign of Risa. It looked like June had managed to sneak out while she was asleep. Why he would do so was a mystery only he could solve, but now Diane had her chance.

She looked around the room and weighed her options. While on board and underway all weapons were stored in the armory, so she couldn't just shoot June. Walter locked all the cutlery away when it wasn't being used. That knocked knives out of the equation.

Diane flexed her fingers. She'd never strangled anyone before. How did it feel, she wondered? She glanced down at her hands and tried to imagine it.

She frowned. She didn't like it at all. It was one thing to kill with tools in the course of her duty. Doing so was impersonal – it was just her job. When she thought about her own two hands committing the act, she balked. Of course she'd been trained to. She'd just never had the opportunity – or orders – to do so before.

The only other weapon she could think of was the weights. She turned and studied them, then hefted a twenty-five pound dumbbell. It would do nicely. All she would have to do was drop it on his chest and the impact alone would be enough to end him. There might not even be much of a mess.

June was still sleeping peacefully when she reached him. The dumbbell was heavy in her grip while she just stared at him. She studied his content expression, the way he sighed in his sleep. His ear twitched and he shifted, drawing his legs up to his chest more.

Diane raised the weight. It would take so little effort on her part. All she had to do was open her hands and it would be done.

She just had to relax her fingers.

Diane frowned. Her fingers weren't opening. She lowered the weight and set it on the floor. Maybe she didn't want to do it like this. Maybe she did want to do this with her own hands.

She knelt down and reached for him. His skin was warm from the artificial sun. She could feel his pulse just under his fingertips. It would be so, so easy to press hard and stop that flow. It would take only a few minutes and it would be over. She was the only one awake right now. His body could be disposed of before anyone was the wiser.

June murmured something in his sleep and turned to her. His eyes blinked open, but he wasn't properly awake. It was debatable whether he saw Diane or just some figment of his dreams.

Her fingers were still on his neck. She traced them up the soft skin, to his hair, and finally to the source of her discomfort. The cat ear twitched under her fingers. She persisted, stroking the soft fur. It reminded her of her childhood friend's cat.

Absently, she stroked around that ear just around the base. June purred happily, his eyes sliding closed again. Diane watched in fascination as he relaxed completely and turned towards her hand. He was completely defenseless. So why couldn't she do it?

Diane picked the weight up and carried it back to the rack. She took extra time to make sure it was properly stowed away, then turned back to June. In just that short time he'd curled up again.

Without really understanding what she was doing she returned to his side. Humans were humans, she reminded herself. Humans had to protect each other from the alien threat. Anything alien, anything that could threaten the cohesiveness of human society, had to be eliminated. It was a fact of life. As a soldier, Diane dealt with those facts every single day.

June wasn't human. He had to be eliminated. It didn't matter that he looked like a child. Dangerous things came in packages of all kinds.

Diane knelt again at his side and stared at him. She paid no mind to the ears, or the tail that was dragging on the ground. For the first time she just stared at... June.

He was small. Diane didn't know if he was just small compared to her or small in general. She reached out hesitantly and brushed the bangs from his forehead. When his eyes weren't open, his face looked so normal.

She sat there for a few moments before sighing. She sat in the other lounge and scowled at the sunlamp that turned on above her head.

Well, damnit. She glared at the lamp as the only convenient outlet for her frustration. Why couldn't she kill June? She raised a hand and stared at her traitorous limb.

There was a sound from next to her and she looked over at the catboy. He sat up and rubbed at his eyes, then looked around until his gaze landed on Diane. He staggered to his feet and crossed the few feet to Diane's chair.

"You're not," she said in disbelief.

He ignored her words and climbed into her lap. Diane didn't know what to do as he made himself comfortable. She stared down at him as he looked up, his eyes half-lidded, and smiled blearily.

"You're pushing it," Diane warned.

June clutched her arm, drew his tail up so it was curled up on her chest, and rested his head on her shoulder. Just that quickly he was out again.

Diane could only stare in disbelief. She raised a hand to his neck again and stroked his spine. She wanted nothing more than to be able to just close her hand on it in one strong movement. If she did it just right, June wouldn't feel a thing.

Even as that thought crossed her mind she knew that she couldn't do it. June was just too, well, innocent. She was trained to protect the innocent from the alien threat. June wasn't quite human – but he wasn't quite inhuman either.

Diane sighed. June was warm against her, comfortable. Even so, she couldn't take care of her nightly duties like this.

It seemed the boy was well and truly out now. Diane was able to manhandle him so she could hook one arm under his knees and cradle his shoulders. The hardest part was keeping her balance when she stood up, but this was handled and she trekked out of the room.

At Risa's door, she couldn't reach the buzzer. She settled instead for kicking it. Hopefully she wouldn't wake up everyone.

It only took a few kicks before Diane heard movement on the other side of the door. She settled June more comfortably in her arms and waited. A few minutes later, minutes filled with increasingly frantic movement, the door slid open.

Risa looked ready to charge out, her hair in disarray and her pajamas surprisingly flowery. She stopped short when she saw Diane, and June. "Uh," she said eloquently.

"You need a lock," Diane said bluntly. "Or a bell."

"A collar," Risa mused, then shook herself awake. "He snuck out. And you haven't hurt him." She didn't seem to quite believe it and she reached out to June. She brushed the hair from his forehead, checked his pulse.

"Can you please invite me in so I can put him down?" Diane asked. "He's not exactly weightless."

Risa stepped aside and let the other woman into her room. Diane stepped in and glanced around before heading for the bed. If she had to guess, this was where June usually slept. The blue fur on the sheets confirmed her suspicions. She used the boy's legs to nudge aside the blankets before settling him down gently. He clung to her shirt, but with patience Diane was able to extricate herself. She hesitated, then pulled the blanket up over his body. He curled up.

Diane looked around the room again. Her eyes settled on the picture on the nightstand and she frowned. There was something plastic about the boy in the picture. She picked up the image and peered at it.

"I didn't know you had a son," she said conversationally. This was her first voyage with Risa. Science and military didn't often mix and they hadn't had much of a chance to converse.

The picture was plucked from her fingers. Diane looked up and saw the sorrow on Risa's face. "You don't have a son," she realized.

Risa gestured to the door. "Let's take this outside," she suggested.

A few minutes later they were settled in the mess hall. Diane got a cup of coffee for herself while Risa made some tea. When they were seated around the table, Risa took a breath.

"Your second guess was right," she said. "I don't have a son."

"So why do you have a picture?" Diane asked. It didn't seem to add up.

Risa hands shook around her mug. "That's a picture of the son I would have had."

Diane frowned. "I don't get it."

"I was pregnant," Risa said wistfully. "Six months. I was still working, but I was so close to maternity leave. My baby… was so close to being able to survive outside the womb."

Diane thought she knew where this was going. She stayed silent, however, as Risa took in a shuddering breath and sipped her tea.

"There was a complication," the medic whispered. 'I started to miscarry. They rushed me to surgery and tried to deliver him, but my baby…" She started to sob.

Diane just waited.

It took a few moments to collect herself, but Risa eventually continued. "He wasn't technically born. I couldn't even call him my child in paperwork. And he… he tore me up on his way out. The doctors had to remove everything." Risa's hand went below the table. Diane could picture the other woman cradling her lower abdomen. "I can't have another baby. I don't have a uterus, or ovaries, or anything."

"So what about the picture?" Diane asked finally.

"A company took my baby's DNA and used a computer to determine what he would look like. They gave me a range of ages to choose from, but any older than one year and the results were too fake." Risa sipped from her tea.

Diane frowned, her mind working. The pieces were finally starting to fall into place. "June," she said after a moment. "That's what you were going to name your son."

Risa nodded. "I agonized over the name. I finally settled on June because... well, he was conceived in June. Unimaginative, I know, but it became rather poetic." There was a soft smile on her face as she stared into memory.

"So you gave the name of your unborn child to an alien boy you found in the middle of a pack of monsters in outer space," Diane mused. She shrugged. "It's as good as I could have come up with."

"I've never thought of another name," Risa admitted. "There wasn't ever a point. Even if I adopted, that child would already have a name."

"Why don't you get a cloned uterus?" Diane asked. "They can clone anything nowadays."

Risa's expression hardened. "Government insurance doesn't cover non-essential cloning," she said tightly. "If I needed a lung or a kidney, they'd shell out for it. Apparently a woman's reproductive system isn't essential. Private insurance won't take me while I'm on government insurance, and I can't afford the procedure on my own. Even if I got out of the military now, the insurance companies would call it a pre-existing condition. I would never be able to save up enough for the procedure until I was too old for it to be useful anyway."

Diane winced sympathetically. "Well, damn. At least you managed to adopt a kid."

Risa blinked at her in confusion. "What do you mean? I don't have a child."

Diane jerked a thumb towards the door. "What do you call that thing currently sleeping in your bed?" She wasn't the most eloquent person. It was hard to put her observation into words. Still, she'd watched June and Risa from afar this past week and she was certain of her impression.

Risa twisted the mug in her hands and frowned. "He's not mine," she protested, though she sounded like she was trying to convince herself. Her eyes fell to the mug. "He won't be around that long anyway," she added in a near-whisper.

"So?" Diane asked. It looked like she was going to have to explain it anyway. Wasn't Risa supposed to be the empathetic one? She drummed her fingers on the table while she tried to sort her feelings on the matter.

"I can't do that again!" Risa shouted. She seemed taken aback by her outburst and shrunk in on herself. "I mean... I gave my baby all my love even before he was ever born. When I lost him I felt like there was this hole in my heart. When I learned that I couldn't ever fill that hole, I learned to deal with it. I just can't…" She swiped at more tears that fell from her eyes. "June is going to die, Diane."

Diane was taken aback. She would have thought the doctor would be optimistic. Didn't Risa have connections? It would be an easy matter for the execution order to repeatedly get lost.

Before the marine could speak, Risa continued. "I don't want him to. I want him to live just like any other boy. If I could sneak him away, hide him, I would. I would resign from my commission right now if it meant I could run away with him."

"So why don't you?" Diane asked.

Risa blinked at her. "What do you mean?"

"Run away. You'll be labeled a deserter, true, and you'll become one of the most wanted people on Earth and beyond." Diane shrugged and looked at the ceiling. She wouldn't mind the kind of rough lifestyle that would result from that course of action. "As long as June lived, though, it would be worth it, right?"

There was a slow nod from Risa's direction. "Yes."

"And if it came down to it, you'd give your own life before you ever had to lose him." Diane returned her gaze to Risa's and saw the resolve in the medic's eyes. She couldn't help the satisfied smirk that spread across her lips.

"Without a moment's thought," Risa agreed.

"Hate to say it, Risa, but it's too late for you." Diane winked knowingly at the startled other. "Everything you just said is exactly what a mother would do for her outcast son. Whether that son was a convicted murderer or an alien, every mother would give anything to see him safe."

Risa just sat there, dumbfounded, for a few moments. Then she laughed. "I didn't expect this from you. No offense, you seemed like a total jarhead."

"I am," Diane agreed. She was a marine through and through. "I just have a few moments."

They sat there in silence for a good few minutes. Risa got up and made another cup of tea, which she promptly stared into.

"What am I going to do?" she whispered at last. "I love him, Diane. Just the thought that he's going to die breaks my heart. He's not my blood, he's not even human, but I love him with all my heart."

"What do you think adoptive parents feel?" the marine asked. "They extend their hearts to children who don't have parents to love them. The love they feel isn't any less real." She reached across the table and patted Risa's shoulder. "Just accept it. You adopted June. You named him and he looks to you before anyone else. You're his mother, just like he's your son."

"He's going to die," Risa insisted. "Maybe not when we get back to Earth. I know I'm going to fight with my heart and my position to keep him alive as long as I can. Eventually, though, I won't be able to justify it. One day he's going to take one final walk and I'm going to lose him."

So Risa wasn't entirely pessimistic. Diane was beginning to wonder. "I hate to break that fairy-tale bubble of yours," she said, "but parents lose their children. Some know ahead of time. Some, like you, only discover this when it actually happens. Just love him while you have him."

"And when he's gone?" Risa asked.

Diane shrugged. "You'll grieve. You'll wonder why your world lost its meaning. Then you'll grow numb, before the grief ambushes you and drags you down again."

"Poetic," Risa said dryly.

"Shut up," Diane retorted. "Eventually, you'll stop crying. You'll start to look back on your memories of June fondly. You'll grow wistful, nostalgic, and appreciate the time that you had. I think your problem, Risa, is that you never got to the third part with the first June. All of him that you have is a picture."

"My son was never born," Risa agreed. Her tea was by now cool enough for her to down in one gulp. "Well, I'd better get back to bed. Thanks for taking care of June earlier."

"You'd better hope he hasn't wandered off again," Diane grinned.

"We'll know where to find him," the medic pointed out. She headed for the door but paused on the threshold. "Diane... thanks."

"Don't mention it," the marine returned. "I may not like aliens, but it's my job to protect mothers and sons. I'll keep you and June safe."

Risa smiled at her and continued on her way. Diane stood and checked the time. She still had many hours until breakfast and then sleep. Now what else was there she could do to occupy her time?

Chapter 13

Risa stumbled into the mess hall half-panicked. Once again, when she woke up, June was missing. How the boy had managed to get out of her room again was a mystery, but that mystery would have to be answered later on. Her only priority right now was to find out where he was and ensure that he was safe.

Diane stared at her, an apple dangling above her head. June was in her lap and reaching for it desperately. "What's got you running around like this so early in the morning?"

Risa glared at June and ignored the marine. The boy finally noticed her and his expression lit up, apple forgotten. "Maggie!" he called cheerfully. When her frown didn't abate, his face fell and his ears went back.

"Go easy on him," Evan advised. It was only then that Risa realized that the rest of the crew was in full witness to her state – still in her pajamas, her hair askew. She hastily patted her hair into some semblance of order and coughed.

"June, come here," she said. Her voice was harsh still and June cringed. She shook her head and took calming breaths. Her fears hadn't come to pass so there was no longer a need for her to act on her panic. June wasn't able to understand her emotions right now and so lashing out at him would be cruel.

"I'm sorry," she said gently. "Come here, June."

June's ears twitched upwards and he slid of out Diane's lap. Risa opened her arms so he could squeeze her tightly, and she brushed the hair from his forehead tenderly. "Don't scare me like that again," she half-begged, half-whispered. "If I woke up and you were dead I don't know what I would do."

"Stop worrying about that!" Evan scolded her.

"Like I said last night, I'll protect him," Diane said. She held the apple up. "June, you forgot your treat."

The boy looked up at the sound of his name. At the sight of the apple, he bolted out of Risa's arms to Diane. This time she handed him the apple without hesitation. He smiled happily and cradled it in his palms.

"Go on," Diane coaxed. "You like them, right?"

June sunk his fangs into the apple, but when he tried to bite down he yelped in pain. Risa was at his side in a second, and between her and Diane they got the apple out of June's mouth. June touched his fangs with a whimper and stared at the apple like it was the thing that had bit him.

"What just happened?" Evan asked. The sympathetic half of the crew had jumped to their feet at June's cry and was watching them warily.

Risa lifted June's chin and checked his teeth. No sign of blood, that was good. She picked up the apple and stared at it with a frown. "That's a good question."

She studied the bite mark, then looked at June's fangs again. "Ah, I got it," she said after a moment. "June can't bite into apples because they're too hard, and the pressure from doing so almost broke his fangs."

"Apple," June repeated in dismay. He looked at the fruit with longing, but at the same time he was visibly touching his fangs with his tongue.

Walter muttered something disparaging under his breath and turned back to his breakfast. Slowly, the rest of the crew settled back down. "Sorry," Diane told Risa. "I didn't mean to hurt him."

"It's fine," Risa dismissed. "I couldn't have guessed that would happen either." She took the apple to the kitchen so she could wash it off. Back in the dining room, she sliced it up and presented it to June. The boy grinned at her and took careful bites out of the slices.

"So, is it casual Friday?" Evan asked Risa with a wink. Risa managed to cover her embarrassment with a shrug.

"It's not even Friday," she retorted. "I'm going to go get dressed. Be good, June."

The boy looked up at his name, but Risa was already out of the room. Despite her nonchalance, she picked up the pace once she was out of sight of the mess hall. She had to trust the crew sometime, but she couldn't help the uncertainty in her gut. Some part of her was screaming that she couldn't leave June alone with them.

Risa rushed to change her clothes and raked her brush through her hair. She struggled with her shoes while she tried to brush her teeth at the same time. Hurry, hurry, her subconscious chanted at her. Hurry or June wouldn't be there when she returned.

She made it back to the mess hall and managed to hide her sigh of relief. June was chomping on his eggs and toast with great fervor while Evan talked to him animatedly. June's word comprehension was growing, but it still wasn't good enough for him to understand Evan's story. Still, from what Risa could hear while she went to get her own breakfast, Evan's childhood made for great storytelling.

"And then," Evan was saying when Risa sat and began eating, "the other team decided to cheat!"

June looked at Risa and smiled. "Hi," he greeted.

"Good morning," Risa returned. She turned her attention to Evan. "So what'd the other team do?"

"They rigged this antigrav machine and put it in the ball," Evan groaned. "Every time one of us tried to grab it, it floated away!"

[130]

Risa pictured it in her head and giggled. "So what happened to the other team?"

"Detention, from what I heard. The league kept the doctored ball so that they could take it around and show the teams what not to do. Wish we could have kept it, though," Evan said wistfully.

Despite the few hostile looks breakfast ended peacefully after that. June watched as Risa collected her plates and followed suit. He dutifully followed her to the trash, pretended to scrape off his plates and set them where Risa pointed.

"He learns quickly," Gerald noted. Risa turned to him and nodded.

"He does, Captain," she agreed. "I have him playing learning games while I work on Darryl's notes and he's beaten many of them already. I wouldn't be surprised if he understands more than we think."

"That's always the case with children," the Captain said fondly. "So what are your plans for today?"

"I'll be working more on the notes," Risa said, tapping her chin while she thought ahead. "I'm also going to try to get him to sit still so I can get more samples. The more I get, I think, the less he'll be poked when he gets to Earth."

"Why does that matter?" Evan asked.

"He hates needles," Risa explained, then told them of how she got her one blood sample. "So, I think it'll be better if I do it," she finished.

"That sounds like a good plan," Gerald affirmed. "Get to it when you're ready, Dr. Magee."

"Yes, sir," Risa said. Her hand snapped up in a salute out of reflex – she might be medical, but she was still military. June caught her attention and she looked over to see him imitating the salute, then frown. He wiggled his fingers as if he didn't quite understand it.

"Come on, June," she called, and he reached for her hand. Risa smiled and squeezed gently. "It's time to get to work."

Once they were safely ensconced in the infirmary, Risa left June to his tablet while she checked the computer. The task she had set to it was complete and she stared at the results.

"This can't be right," she sighed. The screen, however, presented her with its findings without caring that what it displayed was impossible. "That's a high enough dose to put down a small elephant."

She called up the analysis of June's blood and stared at it for a while. June shook her out of it when he tapped her shoulder. "More," he said, tablet held out for her to take.

"Did you finish that one?" she asked. She closed the current learning game and found the next one in the series. "Here you go." To her surprise, it was one focused on basic reading. "You've gotten that far already?"

June beamed at her and retreated to the bed to continue playing. Risa returned to the computer and grudgingly agreed with its findings. On the surface June was a normal boy, but there were some elements hiding in his chemical makeup that skewed things.

It also promised to make his life harder in the future, but Risa put that aside. She went into her medicine stores and located the drug she was after. The dose that was called for was almost enough to empty her inventory of it. She had enough to knock June out once, and then enough for a few normal doses, and that was it.

If only she could use needles, she lamented. The drug she had was meant to be administered orally. She had plenty of the intravenous kind. If only she could put June on the normal anesthetic.

Still, it was what she had. This just meant that her plan to have these tests spread out over days wasn't feasible. She'd have to get everything done while she had June knocked out.

She poured the medicine into a glass and carried it to June. The boy looked up at her with a smile. "What is?" he asked, pointing to the glass.

"It's something to make you sleep," she explained. She didn't know how much of it June would understand, but she kept her voice gentle. "It's going to taste bad but you have to drink all of it, okay?"

"Sleep," June repeated. He put his hands together and pretended to rest his head against them like a pillow. "Is sleep?"

"Yes," Risa said. She felt warmth in her heart – June was learning so fast! "You won't feel a thing, and you'll wake up in a few hours."

June took the glass and stared into it. "No sleep," he protested. "Play."

"You have to," Risa told him. "You can play when you wake up, okay?" Though whether he'd want to was a different story. "Drink it all," she instructed. She held her nose and mimed drinking quickly. "Just like that."

June took a sip of the medicine and make a face at the bitter taste. "Bad," he complained.

Risa mimed again. "Just like that," she repeated.

June squeezed his nose shut and gulped the medicine down. He came up for air with a disgusted moan. "Taste bad," he said, raising his eyes to Risa's. "Sleep now?"

"It'll take a minute," she said. Enough time for him to wash the taste from his mouth. She grabbed a bottle of water and handed it to him. "Just a sip. Don't want to dilute the medicine too much."

June managed a swallow of water before the drug started to take effect. Risa cradled his head and helped him settle back against the bed. "It's all right," she said softly. She stroked his hand and forehead. "Just relax and sleep."

June fought the medicine, his eyelids fluttering rapidly. Risa leaned down and kissed his forehead. "It's okay," she assured him. "I'll be here the whole time. Just sleep."

Chapter 14

June smiled at her before his eyes finally slipped closed. Risa waited a few moments to be sure he was really out, then turned to the computer and set the room for surgery mode. This meant that the room would be sealed and sterilized – anyone wanting in would have to use the intercom. The screen split itself into various windows. June's vitals were steady, and Risa's pre-prepared checklist sat waiting. If anything went wrong, an alarm would sound.

Her first order of business was getting June ready for the procedure. She carefully took off his shirt and folded it neatly at the bedside. After a moment's hesitation she also took off his shorts, leaving him only in his boxers. She had it in mind to do a thorough exam once she was done, but she was still uncertain. It depended on how long it took her to finish her planned task.

While Risa waited for the sterilization to finish she dug into her cabinets for supplies. She set June up with an I.V. It pained her to stick him with the needles he hated but he was oblivious. She got the saline up and then attached the standard anesthetic. She wouldn't give it to him until later, when the oral medicine was about to wear off. There was no sense in risking an overdose.

She winced at the sight of the biopsy needle. This was the real reason June was now sleeping. She was going to sample every organ she could manage to reach with the needle. There were a few that she would have to get really invasive for.

The computer beeped. The room and everything in it was now sterile. Risa pulled on her surgical mask, donned her gloves, and began her work. Every time the biopsy needle pierced June's skin, a little weight settled in her heart.

Doing this made her feel guilty. She loved June and never imagined she could do this to her son. The more she hurt him the worse she felt. Yet, she rationalized as she sealed and marked the current sample, if it wasn't her doing it, it would be worse for June. Biopsies were normally performed with the patient awake and aware of everything. To have June awake for this, tied down and able to see the needle, feel the pain of it striking deep into his body – Risa shuddered at the thought. She could imagine his screams and sobs echoing and had to pause.

June stirred and Risa left her thoughts behind. She hooked the anesthetic to his I.V. and waited until he relaxed into unconsciousness again. With a new pair of gloves on she resumed her work. There was no time to think of anything but getting the task done.

Risa finally finished with the needle and discarded it gladly. She looked at the I.V. and debated whether or not she'd have enough time to do her planned physical exam. She did. So, she turned to the computer and brought up a list of Darryl's son's injuries.

Upon first glance, June's body was pristine. It was only when Risa peered closely that she saw the imperfections. A scar on his chest, winding its way around from his sternum to his spine. White lines on his wrists and ankles. A healed puncture wound, visible on his hip only when his boxers were pulled down. There were countless other marks adorning his body as well.

These marks matched up exactly with the reports. No matter how impossible it seemed, June couldn't have been grown in a laboratory environment. The scars were far too faded and worn. Darryl had really twisted his son's body into what June was now.

Risa unhooked the I.V. and dressed June. It wouldn't take him long to wake up but he would feel horrid once he did. Risa dragged her computer chair over to June's bedside and took his hand in hers. She stroked his forehead and waited for him to wake again. She knew that she should be writing up her findings, but that was somehow less important than comforting the boy.

The fact that she had to do this to him at all made her sad. June didn't deserve to be thought of only as a lab animal. The attention on him should be focused on his remarkable cognitive development, not on the biological particulars that made him tick.

Risa sighed. This was what her superiors wanted. It was her job to analyze Darryl's genetic research. The fact that June was a wonderfully cheerful young child was lost on her bosses.

June stirred and groaned. "It's okay," Risa told him. She squeezed his hand comfortingly. "You'll feel a bit of pain but it won't last too long. It should be gone tomorrow."

The boy whimpered and clutched Risa's hand. "Maggie," he whispered.

"I'm here," she assured him. "Does it hurt?"

"Hurt," June repeated, then groaned again. His hand tenderly touched the skin above his liver – one of the many places Risa had biopsied. He hissed in pain and looked at Risa, his eyes confused and scared.

"It's okay to say if it hurts," Risa told him softly. "I'm sorry I had to do this to you."

"Hurts," June agreed.

They stayed like that a few moments before Risa had an idea. "I know what might make you feel better," she told him. "Let's go to the gym. The sun lamps should feel good, right?"

It turned out June couldn't stand. Risa helped him back down and went to the intercom. "Evan," she called into it, then waited.

She didn't have to wait long. "What's up, Risa?" the marine's voice asked.

"Could you come to the infirmary?" Risa asked.

He was there in a matter of minutes. With the surgical protocols disabled, he was able to stroll right in. "What can I do for you?" he asked.

"Can you carry June?" the medic asked. "He's just had a lot of things done to him and he's not feeling well. I think a little sun should help him."

"What sort of things?" Evan asked, but he obligingly lifted June gently out of the infirmary bed.

"I had to poke him with a lot of needles. Be careful, he's in a lot of pain." Risa hovered as Evan carted June to the gym and settled him gently onto the lightly padded lounge. June protested a bit when he was set down, but immediately quieted when the sun lamp turned on.

Risa settled onto the floor next to the chair and took June's hand again. The boy looked up at her, still so weak and worn out that his ears didn't even twitch. "Maggie," he said again and gripped her hand hard. He tugged on it until Risa stood, then tried to pull her down onto the lounge with him.

"I won't fit," Risa protested.

A clicking sound attracted her attention and both Risa and June turned to see Evan unhooking the second lounge from the floor. He unceremoniously lifted Risa from her feet, settled the lounge against June's, and put Risa down gently on it.

"He's a scared kid wanting his mother," Evan explained to the startled medic. "My brother used to sleep with me when he was in pain too. It helps."

June was already snuggling against Risa. He clutched her hand to his chest and relaxed. "Maggie," he sighed contently.

Rise gently wrapped her arm around him. "It's okay," she said softly while she rubbed his back soothingly.

He was still in pain, she could tell by the tightness around his eyes, but at least he wasn't making pained noises anymore. The sun lamp was warm and relaxing. "A nap wouldn't hurt," she murmured, already slipping into sleep. Even more comforting was having her son warm and alive in her arms. How often had she dreamt of this?

A tail wound itself around her waist and she smiled. June was hers. She was his. She would raise him as long as she could. If she could raise him long enough to watch him grow into a strong adult...

She fell asleep with that thought in her head.

Walter was on his way to the bathroom when, on his way past the gym, he heard the most undignified sounds coming from his shipmates. He paused, his bladder warring with his curiosity. His bladder won out.

Fortunately, the sounds hadn't stopped when he returned. He peered into the room and saw the rest of the crew gathered around the lounge chairs. Renee was doing most of the cooing – cooing! – while the rest of the crew was snickering quietly behind their hands.

"What's going on?" Walter asked. He was immediately shushed and he blinked in confusion.

"They're so cute," Renee whispered, pointing at the lounge chairs.

Walter knew just who they were talking about but he walked up to the group anyway. Sure enough Risa was fast asleep on the lounge with the alien boy curled up in her arms. The boy blinked at him as he walked up but otherwise didn't move.

The position managed to mask the boy's tail, and his ears were hidden by Risa's hand on his head. With those inhuman features obscured, the picture in front of Walter was undeniably cute. June's eyes moved to look at each of them, but in the shadows their slits couldn't be seen well.

"What brought this on?" Walter asked despite himself.

"June's not feeling well," Evan explained, "and Risa must have been exhausted. She passed out right away."

"It's cute," Renee sighed again.

"I thought you were a man," Walter grumbled under his breath. Still, it was an adorable picture. June apparently decided to ignore them and buried his face in Risa's arm.

"We need a picture of this," Gerald murmured. "For posterity."

"Did anyone bring a camera with them?" Evan asked.

"Not me," Gary said wistfully. Walter looked at him in shock, and the janitor reddened. "What? He might be an alien kid but this is just too cute of a picture."

Walter rolled his eyes. He could only take so much cuteness. "I'll go look for the camera," he volunteered. "I didn't realize this was a ship full of girls," he added under his breath as he walked out.

"We're just secure in our masculinity!" Evan called after him – quietly, of course.

Walter walked to the mess hall to look for the ship's camera. On his way he passed Risa's office and paused. Both the door to the infirmary and the cabinet containing the ship's store of medicine had been left wide open. It was uncharacteristic of Risa to be so unorganized.

Walter only paused a moment, and there was no one as a witness. Hands stuffed in his pocket he continued on and snagged the camera.

Chapter 15

This ship was starting to feel too much like a passenger liner than a military ship, Gary grumbled. He was mopping up yet another unknown material in the hallways – this time outside of the crew cabins. With most of the crew looking out for June the alien boy was running freely about the ship.

On the one hand, his odds of catching June by himself had skyrocketed. On the other, the boy's disappearance would be noticed far sooner. Gary had to plan his moves carefully. Jump the gun and he'd be found out.

Still, there were only two days left before they got to Earth. Gary's window of opportunity was rapidly closing. Soon he'd have to act, regardless of the consequences. June had to be taken care of before it was too late.

Gary plopped his mop back in the bucket and sighed. Why did his job have to be so hard?

There was a tug on his sleeve and he turned to look at its source. June beamed up at him, ears perky and his tail twitching energetically. "Gary!" the boy greeted cheerfully.

The world didn't work like this, the janitor thought. He stared at the boy he was thinking about only a second ago in shock. June frowned and stepped back.

"Ah, sorry," Gary said hastily. He smiled at the boy. "You just surprised me. What did you want?"

June twisted his expression into one of intense concentration. "Maggie says... need bleach," he said carefully. "Mess."

Gary sighed and kneaded his forehead. "What'd you spill this time?" he asked.

June didn't answer, though it wasn't as if Gary expected one. The catboy was speaking – haltingly, it was true, and his sentence structure left much to be desired – but anything more than short statements was out of the question. At least this was the opportunity Gary had been waiting for.

"I'll get the bleach," Gary agreed. "Just come with me a minute, okay?" He walked over to his cabin and opened the door. June hesitated before entering the room too.

Gary's room wasn't much. It was bare, with hardly a personal touch to be seen. It was better that way. There was nothing to incriminate him. He kicked his pajamas from the night before out of the way and gestured for the boy to sit in the lone chair.

"What is?" June asked. Gary walked up behind him and reached over him to bring his personal computer screen to life. A few taps and the webcam was active. Another tap and a connection to Earth was opened.

"It's a phone," Gary answered. June wouldn't understand, but it wouldn't do to not reward his curiosity. "There's someone who's been wanting to meet you."

"Meet?" June repeated, looking between the screen and Gary's face. "What is meet?"

"It means to see, to walk up to and greet," the janitor replied. "After my friend meets you, you'll go to meet Risa, right?"

"Maggie," June agreed with a nod. "Meet Maggie!"

A voice interrupted them. "So this is the boy."

June jumped and looked at the screen. Gary patted his head between his ears. "It's okay, June. It won't hurt you."

He turned his attention to the woman on the screen. She was older, creeping past her fifties into her sixties, and only a few traces of pale brown remained in her long gray hair. Her face was lined with the evidence of one who spent many years in her youth smiling. Now, her vibrant cerulean eyes were somber as they looked at them from many millions of miles away. She wasn't dressed in the military uniforms that were all

June knew. Her suit was a subdued green, more forest than emerald.

She was a civilian – though June wouldn't understand that distinction. All he would know, Gary expected, was that this woman was dressed differently. If Gary and this woman couldn't take care of June, all he would ever know was the cruel hand of the military.

That wasn't an acceptable option.

"Yes, this is him," Gary told the woman. He crouched next to June so the woman could see him as well. "It's been a while, Isobel."

"Too long. There isn't much time left." Isobel Barclay tore her eyes away from June and looked at Gary sternly. "Why did you wait until now to contact me?"

"I couldn't get June alone. I didn't want to call any attention to myself and blow my cover." Gary looked over at the boy, whose eyes were darting from Gary to Isobel in confusion. "June?" he asked.

"What is?" June asked helplessly, hand reaching to the screen and tracing Isobel's cheeks. "Don't…"

"What's wrong with him?" Isobel asked. "We don't have much data on our end. Risa's reports have all been entirely factual."

"He's young," Gary sighed. "Not just physically I mean. Mentally he's… I don't know, about a toddler's age? Whatever Darryl did to him, it rendered him mentally an infant. He's learning, but some things he just can't understand yet."

Ignoring Isobel for the moment, Gary took June's hand and squeezed it. "Hey," he said softly. "Don't worry about it. Isobel is a nice woman, okay? She's going to help you."

"Izbel," June repeated, his eyes fixed on Gary. "Is… Izbel?" he asked, pointing at the screen.

"Yes, that's Isobel," Gary confirmed. "She's been wanting to meet you for a while."

"Meet Izbel," June said with a frown. "Izbel… not…" He shook his head and gestured to Gary. "Not!" he insisted.

Without knowing what June meant there was no way to placate him. Gary smiled softy at him instead and ruffled his hair. "It's all right. Don't worry about it okay?"

June nodded. "Okay."

Gary turned to Isobel. "I'll be right back. We've been gone too long."

Once June was on his way with a tightly sealed bottle of bleach in his hand, Gary returned to Isobel. "Sorry about that."

"It's fine. You didn't have to wait to get him here to talk to me about him, you know," Isobel chastised him.

Gary chuckled and tried to think of how to explain his reasons. "Everyone on board… they hated June from the moment they saw him," he started. "But when they interacted with him, got to know him, that hate went away. It's because of that that I wanted you to meet him. Just hearing about him isn't enough.

People seem to need to talk with him before they grow to like him."

"Risa didn't need any of that, from what you've sent me," Isobel pointed out.

"She fell in love with him from the first moment she met him," Gary agreed. "Usually you think that about romantic couples, you know? But that's what happened. Risa met June and couldn't seem to help wanting to take care of him. Renee has a word for that: moe. It's some kind of weird Japanese word but the way he describes it makes it the perfect way to describe June."

"I'll have to look it up," Isobel nodded. "Is Risa going to be a problem in this?"

"If we try to separate them, she will be," Gary said immediately. "She's even gone so far as to start calling him her son."

"Don't say that like it's a bad thing," Isobel mused. "Parental bonds are a funny thing. Have you ever heard of stories from Earth's own animals? Lions adopting gazelles as family, a raven raising a kitten to a full adult. If Risa is calling June her son, it just means that they've formed that mother-child bond."

"Of course. I'm sorry, I didn't mean it like that." Gary sighed and sat back in his chair. "I'm just worried about her. She won't take it well if we spirit June away without her."

"Of course she won't. No good mother would. You have to think of things from our point of view, though," Isobel cautioned. "Risa loves June. Does that mean she would love just any alien that crossed her path?"

"Doubt it. On the trip here she made her opinions very clear – quite mainstream, really. They're all bad, kill them all, the works." Gary understood where Isobel was going with her thought process now and nodded. "So even though she's willing to take care of June, not even a proper alien but still reviled, it doesn't mean she's on our side."

"Right. We've already gotten our defenses of him in order. We're going to argue that the traditional definition of 'alien' doesn't apply to him." Isobel paused. "I didn't realize that that was the boy's name."

"Ah, Risa named him," Gary said. "It's not like we could ask Darryl what it was."

"His proper name isn't in the system. Darryl purged all of the records," Isobel lamented. "I suppose it's a good enough name. It's a peaceful one."

"So, what's going to happen?" Gary prompted. Isobel shook her head and cleared her throat.

"First, there's going to be a meeting between the military heads and scientific ones. All of them agree that June must be eliminated – he started off human but he's quite obviously not anymore. The argument is going to be over when." Isobel tapped her fingers. "Our contacts in the scientific wings are going to try to argue that June is human and what was done to him wasn't his fault. Then they'll drag out that 'alien' used to mean 'not from Earth', not how it's usually applied now. If all else fails, we have a way of getting him out before they can kill him."

"And what about Risa?" Gary asked. He knew that she couldn't go with June. The risk to their group was too great. Still, he couldn't help his twinge of guilt when he thought of her. She was happy, completely unlike the cool professional he'd met on the trip to Darryl's ship. To lose June would devastate her.

Isobel looked guilty too. "I would love it if we could reunite her with June at a later date," she said after a moment. "I wouldn't ever want to rip a mother and son apart, but we just can't risk it. Once she learns why we did it, she might forgive us."

"I hope so." Gary wanted nothing more at this moment to just be back on Earth so this could all be done and over with. It was a heavy weight on his heart, this planning. He would be a good coworker and comfort Risa after June was gone. It would just hurt him to not be able to tell her just where June was.

The idealistic part of his brain was rebellious. Why couldn't Risa know her son was alive and well? It was a hell that she just didn't have to go through. Sure she couldn't see him without exposing the whole group to the public. Just knowing he was alive would help. She'd understand their reasons. Maybe one day they could be reunited.

It was an unrealistic dream. If Risa knew that June lived she'd tear apart the whole world looking for him. That would drag too many government agencies down on their heads.

"Still, June is a remarkable boy," Isobel continued. Her voice dragged Gary out of his thoughts. "You said that two weeks ago he couldn't speak a word?"

"He still pronounces some things wrong but yeah. Risa said she has him playing learning games." Gary thought back to the first time he met June. "Two weeks ago he was just repeating what he heard. Today he asked me for bleach because there was a mess."

"And he asked you about me," Isobel said. "This is quite remarkable. It's like somehow his brain is trying to compensate for his body's age by allowing him to learn faster."

"That's way over my head," Gary admitted. "I'm just on this cruise as a janitor, you know that. Back on Earth you can explain to me just what you mean then."

"Agreed." Isobel checked her watched. "It's time for me to go. There's still so much to do about June. So many things can go wrong at this point and any of them will cost him his life."

"I'll contact you with any new information," Gary promised.

So. That was the plan. Just sit and wait, and break Risa's heart at the end of it all. Gary thought back to the events a few days prior and had an idea.

Maybe Risa couldn't keep June. She could still keep a reminder of him.

Chapter 16

Walter bringing out a generously-sized cake the night before their return to Earth was a shock to the whole crew. He nearly dropped it on Diane trying to get it to the table, but once it was there Risa stared at it. "What's this?" she asked, torn between suspicion and glee.

"It's a cake," Evan said dryly. He was already reaching to taste the frosting, but a glare from Walter stopped him.

"I can see that," Risa said impatiently. "I meant, what for?"

"It's for June," Walter explained. He vanished into the kitchen and came out with a knife and plates. As he passed them around, he continued. "I mean, he's a cute kid, so I figured he should get a birthday cake."

"It's not his birthday," Risa pointed out. When was June's birthday, anyway? While she perused his files she was more focused on his physical features. She hadn't paid any attention to his date of birth at all. All she knew was that her estimation of his age was right. He was twelve years old.

Already old enough, if he'd been a normal boy, to start thinking of girls as cute. Risa lamented the years that he'd spent as a vegetable. She cursed the unknown months that he'd been awake and neglected by Darryl. Hopefully, she thought, these two weeks were enough to keep him cheerful.

She couldn't help but miss the milestones she never saw. June might act young but he wasn't. She would never see his first steps. His first word, his own name, might well have been his third or fourth. There was so much she'd missed that she would never get the chance to do again, not with June.

Yet, she was grateful. Any time spent with him was a joy. She couldn't help the impulse to reach over and give him a hug. He returned it with a cheerful smile.

"Birthday or not, we always love cake," Evan declared. "Cut it!"

The cake was sliced up and the pieces passed around. It was a red velvet that, when Risa bit into it, exploded with flavor. The frosting with it was a bit bitter, like strawberry cough syrup, and after her first bite she scraped the rest of the frosting off. The cake itself was chocolaty and delicious and melted on her tongue.

"It's so good," she enthused. "What's your secret?"

Walter was only eating the cake too. "Not much. We got a lot of stuff off of Darryl's ship so I was able to have fun with it. I made the frosting myself. It's buttercream with strawberries. I don't really like strawberries but the rest of you do."

Risa didn't have the heart to tell him that she didn't like the frosting. Instead, she smiled and turned to June. "Do you like it?" she asked.

June nodded enthusiastically. "Good!" He had frosting all over his face and Risa laughed.

"You're supposed to eat it," she teased. When she looked up in search of a napkin, she paused. The rest of her crewmates were falling asleep in their chairs. "Is everyone all right?" she asked, reaching to the nearest one and checking for a pulse. Diane's heart thumped steadily under her fingers but she was undeniably out of it.

"What could have done this?" she asked, already standing to attend to her crew. A chair scraping across the floor startled her.

"They'll be fine," Walter said calmly. "Just a bit of sleeping medicine in the frosting. You should have had some, too. It would have been so much easier on you both if you had just slept the next few hours away." His eyes slid to June, who set down his fork slowly. "I suppose I shouldn't have expected a monster to be affected by human medicine."

"June," Risa called, and the boy came to her without hesitation. She pushed him behind her and fumbled for something, anything, to protect him with.

[155]

"So this is why you baked the cake. Not to be nice to June, but to take out the crew so you could kill him."

"It has to be done," Walter insisted. He pointed at June. "Just look at him! He's not human anymore. I know you say he is, but you can see it just by looking at him. No human has those ears. No human has a tail!"

"Actually, some babies are born with tails," Risa interjected. Then she shook her head. "Anyway, that's beside the point. June's just a child! Killing him is wrong, human or not."

"We kill infants all the time," Walter dismissed. "Where does veal come from? Even eating eggs is a form of infanticide." He raised the knife he'd used to cut the cake. "Just stand aside, Doctor. It won't take much. I don't want to hurt a fellow human."

"I won't let you!" Risa shouted. She backed away with June still behind her. She had no weapon, so what could she do? Even so, abandoning June was unthinkable. "You have to get through me. I won't let you kill my son."

"Your son?" Walter repeated incredulously, then laughed. It was a long laugh, deep with a hint of mania. "You'd claim that thing as family? You know what aliens have done to our society. You'd really ally yourself with those monsters?"

"I don't care about aliens. June isn't an alien!" Risa insisted. "He's just a little boy with a father that turned him into a hybrid against his will. Darryl's already dead, there's no one left to punish for that crime."

Walter shrugged. "So be it. When our superiors hear what went on, they'll praise me for killing you too."

He lunged forward, knife in hand. Risa shoved June to the side and followed. She was just fast enough – the knife tore through her jacket but left her skin intact. June cried out in fear and clung to Risa, his eyes focused on the knife blade that sought his heart.

"Maggie!" the boy whimpered. Risa clutched him close.

"I won't let you do this," Risa warned. She had to gulp in air and it felt like her heart was going to beat out of her chest. Adrenaline was a wonderful thing, she thought dazedly.

"There's no letting to be had," Walter dismissed. "You're defenseless."

Risa eyed the door to the hallway and nudged June. He followed her every step as she circled the table, putting the rest of the crew between her and Walter. "You don't have the guts to go through with it," she tried. Arguing with him was going nowhere. "When it comes down to it, you won't be able to hurt him. Then what will you do? You'll have killed me and June will still be alive. I'll be laughing from the grave when they sentence you to die too."

A few more steps. Only a few until she could make a dash for freedom. June's whimpering broke the silence of the ship as she and Walter glared at each other.

"Just you watch," the cook said. He leaped at Risa, knife outstretched, but this time the medic had other plans. She caught the hand with the knife and grappled for control of it.

"Run, June!" she cried as she struggled. The boy hesitated, looking between her and the unconscious crew. "Run!" she screamed again. "Get to my cabin and lock yourself in. Don't let anyone else in!"

"Maggie," June whimpered before turning and fleeing down the hallway.

"Now it's just you and me," Risa said in relief. Now she could focus all of her attention on keeping the sugar-encrusted knife out of her vital areas. Walter was strong, but in his blind rage he seemed to have forgotten every ounce of military training.

All it took was a twist of his wrist and a shift of her body weight and the knife was hers. Risa hefted it and watched Walter warily. "Just give up," she pleaded. "I won't tell anyone else about what you tried to do. I promise. Just leave June alone."

"I can't," Walter said, and his voice was filled with regret. "I'm sorry, Risa."

When he charged her this time he had the full use of his hands. He shoved Risa off balance and pinned her to the floor with all of his weight. With his legs pinning hers she couldn't kick. Risa lashed out with the knife, but when he wrapped his hands around her throat her aim went off.

Her thoughts slowed. All her attention became focused on the breaths she couldn't take. Attempting to breathe made her head throb and the world greyed out.

She couldn't die here, she thought. June needed her. If she wasn't there he'd die. She couldn't let that happen. June was her son. June had to live!

It took great effort to focus her thoughts. The knife was still in her hand. She shifted it and tried to peer through the gray. Walter's eyes were focused on her face. His expression was gleefully homicidal. He was enjoying choking the life from her.

Risa lashed out. She didn't have any intention of killing him. A minor wound she could treat later, when he was in handcuffs and unable to do anything to June. Right now all she wanted was for him to release her. Only a few seconds left.

She felt more than saw the knife strike home. The pressure around her throat eased and she took great big gulps of air. Color returned to the world slowly, though all she could hear was her own pounding heartbeat.

She didn't take the time to see how badly Walter was injured. She turned and fled. "June!" she whispered, her aching throat making the words hoarse. "June, where are you?"

"Maggie," he whimpered. She saw him cowering in the doorway to the infirmary. When they locked eyes he rushed right into her arms. He was alive, she thought as she squeezed him weakly.

"Risa!" Walter's angry voice echoed through the ship. Risa shoved June into the infirmary and locked the door. Only she and Gerald had the code to this door. Walter wouldn't be able to get them in here.

"It's okay," Risa soothed June. She put the red-stained blade on her desk and looked her son over. He wasn't hurt, that was a relief. "He can't get you now. Don't worry."

June clung to her. "Okay," he said, though his voice was still frightened. His expression turned worried and he touched her throat. "Hurts?"

"Only a little," she assured him. In reality her throat burned and throbbed but she didn't want to worry him. "Don't worry. It's okay."

They both jumped at the thud from outside the door. "You know he has to die!" Walter screamed. "No alien can be allowed to live! They all have to be exterminated!"

Risa ignored him. She shed her tattered jacket and picked up her white lab coat instead. "Don't think about him," she told June. "Just think of a game to play. We'll play when the rest of the crew wakes up, how's that?"

She ushered June to the bed and crawled up on it. He immediately followed and wrapped himself in her arms, still shivering from fear. Risa settled the lab coat over his shoulders and stroked his hair soothingly. Her fingers didn't discriminate between hair and fur and she rubbed his laid-back ears too.

"They'll kill us all!" Walter shouted. "They'll kill us just like they killed my brother! They claim our ship shot at theirs first but I know what really happened. Aliens can't stand to let us live so when they came across a human ship they shot it out of the sky! My brother died at their hands in a ball of fire. I've seen the footage so many times that I can tell you exactly how it happened. Aliens have to die!"

"You're not an alien," Risa whispered to June. "You're my boy. I'll protect you until the day I die. I won't let anyone hurt you."

Walter's cries eventually ceased. June's shivering stopped. Risa sang quietly to him, lullabies and top hits that she couldn't remember half of the words to. Her throat made her voice scratchy and rough but that didn't matter. Bit by bit, June relaxed against her.

After a long length of time, a few hours perhaps, June looked up at her. "Maggie," he said and touched her throat again. "Hurts." He touched his chest and smiled at her. "Okay."

"I'll sing as long as you want me to," she whispered. Her throat really didn't appreciate it, but seeing June smile was worth it. "Just relax and sleep. When the crew wakes up they'll come find us. Walter will be taken care of."

June settled back down. Risa settled back against the wall and waited. There was no way she was going to sleep, not until she knew Walter was out of the picture. Despite her surety that only Gerald could get in, some part of her just couldn't relax.

She spent the night like that, June curled up in her arms and sleeping soundly. She threaded her fingers through his hair and stared at the ceiling. It was hard to not think of the inevitable repercussions of tonight's events.

All that mattered, she told herself time after time, was June. He was alive in her arms, so warm and real that it made her want to cry from relief. He was alive, and anything that happened was secondary to that.

"I love you," she whispered to her son. "I love you so much, June."

He shifted in her arms and mumbled something incoherent.

Hours later she was disturbed from a trance by the door sliding open. Gerald stepped into the room, his eyes sliding from the bloody knife on the desk to her and June on the bed. "Dr. Magee," he said evenly.

"Captain," Risa returned. Everything was going to be all right. She felt relief, but it was dampened by sheer exhaustion. "Where's Walter? Did you take care of him?"

"Walter's dead," Gerald said. "We found him outside the door. He's probably been dead for hours."

Risa tightened her hold on June. "That can't be," she said weakly. "He was alive and trying to kill June, and I had no choice but to fight back. I didn't cut him that deeply, just enough to get him off, and he was alive when he chased us here."

"So he was alive the last time you saw him?" Gerald asked.

Risa told him everything that had happened the night before. Gerald inspected the very visible bruises on her neck from her strangulation and listened intently to every word she said. Once she was done, he tapped his chin and thought.

"You know there's nothing to corroborate your story," he said regretfully. "I believe you, but there's no telling what the military police are going to say."

"I understand," Risa said miserably. Her brain was still wrapping itself around her new identity – murderer. She'd killed someone. She'd gone medical so she wouldn't have to kill anyone.

That didn't matter now, Risa told herself. All she had to focus on was one fact: June was safe. She'd rather see anyone else dead instead of him.

"Get some sleep," Gerald told her. "It's been a long night. We'll wake you before it's time to dock so you have a few last minutes with June."

"Yes, Captain," Risa agreed. She slid out of the bed onto shaky legs, her muscles protesting after their long hours of disuse. June roused enough to follow her out of the room, still-bleary eyes warded from the grisly view by a remorseful Renee and Evan.

"We'll take care of him," Renee told her softly. "We'll try not to let him get hurt."

Risa nodded, too tired to speak. She tried not to look at Walter's grey body but it was no use. His eyes were open and unseeing, his face locked into a wrathful expression. Blood from his left side was invisible on his black uniform, seeming to appear suddenly from places that hadn't been hurt. Red ribbons had dribbled down his leg and across the floor, finally pooling where he'd lied down and died.

She was too tired to be properly sick. Walter wasn't her first dead body, but he was her first, hopefully only, kill. She'd had people die under her hands, but those others she'd tried with all her heart to save. This was a different feeling.

June woke fully as they made it to the showers. He knew by now to go to their room and fetch other clothes. By the time he came back, Risa had already shed her blood-spattered clothes and was under the warm spray.

She didn't turn to him lest he see something he shouldn't. "Take your shower," she told him. Spending the night in the infirmary had made them both miss their nightly shower.

June made an affirming noise and retreated to the privacy shower. Risa focused on the spots of bloods she found on her body – only a few drops, Walter hadn't had enough time to bleed on her too much. She knew it was all in her head but it felt like those innocent drops of rust-red burned. They were a brand, she thought miserably. Even washed away she could still feel them on her skin. They were the mark of her crime.

She couldn't help the tears that streamed down her cheek. She checked the curtain to make sure June couldn't see. She didn't want to worry him about something that wasn't his fault. She could see the curtain rustling as June scrubbed his body, but there was no sign that he would emerge soon. He was very fastidious about cleaning his ears and tail.

It was a challenge to stifle her sobs. They were part sorrow, part relief – Walter was dead, dead, dead, but June was oh-so-alive. Those feelings warred with each other while Risa cried.

Even on board a ship water couldn't stay warm forever, as June had found on his first day. The cold shock against her body snapped Risa out of her grief and she fumbled to shut off the water. She hurried to dry and dress before June's water also went cold.

June's dismayed cry sounded just as she pulled her shirt on. She watched him scramble out of the way and flail for the knob to turn the water off. She couldn't help smiling at him despite the weight in her heart. "You're silly," she told him fondly.

He toweled his tail off first before gently squeezing the water from his hair. He then turned his head upside down so the water could drain out of ears. Risa impulsively grabbed another towel and wrapped it around him with a laugh. He shrieked in surprise but it was a laughing sound as well.

Risa's clothes were soaked again after their impromptu wrestling match. She made sure every inch of June's skin was dry before she released him with a laugh and let him dress. "Go get breakfast," she instructed him with one last pat on the head. "I'll be along after a while."

June giggled and dashed out. Diane had to jump out of the way or else get bowled over. "He's in a good mood," the marine noted. Her voice was somber when she looked at Risa. "I just wanted to check on you. I know killing someone isn't a pleasant experience."

"I'm fine," Risa answered softly. With June gone there was nothing to distract her from the sorrow in her heart. "As long as June's, alive I'm fine."

Diane nodded. "Well, even though I slept through the night, technically I had night watch last night. I feel jetlagged."

"At least you're getting over it now," Risa tried to joke. She really didn't feel it. Diane shrugged and stripped. "I used that one and June used the privacy one," she added, pointing to the showers without hot water.

"Thanks." The marine took care of her business without fanfare. Despite the exhaustion Risa felt, she couldn't help her next question.

"How many have you killed?" she asked, raising her voice over the water.

Diane shrugged. "Too many for me to remember. Some human, some alien, some civilians. Most of them I meant to kill, but civilians always get me. I hate when I accidentally take them out. It makes me angry."

"Walter definitely is - wasn't a civilian," Risa murmured softly. "How do you get over the guilt?"

"Just focus on what you killed for," Diane advised. "I kill to protect innocent people, to defend our nation and planet from threats. Some human settlements aren't exactly cozy. Lots of people are equating our relationship with them to the American Revolution, the British and their American colonies. Sometimes some of those settlements aren't too friendly so they send in the muscle to knock some sense into them. When I kill humans for that, I feel torn – they're fighting for what they believe, but they're dangerous. They could hurt people I care about."

"So you kill them to protect what's precious to you," Risa agreed. She clutched her waterlogged heart, though in her mind's eye it was coated in red. "I would have died to protect June. I'm glad I didn't. I just wish Walter would have listened to reason."

"You can't change what he did, or why he did it. Just focus on June," Diane advised. She finished in the shower and wrapped her hair up, the girliest thing Risa had seen from her yet. "It's going to hurt, don't get me wrong. You'll never forget it. Still, it'll get better eventually."

"It shouldn't," Risa murmured. "Thanks, Diane," she said louder. "I think I'm going to try to sleep."

"Not going to eat?" the marine asked. Her expression was one of understanding despite the question.

"I don't think I could manage," Risa replied honestly.

With that, she left the room. She went to her cabin and changed – June, she realized ruefully, had grabbed her uniform instead of her sleeping clothes. She knew she shouldn't sleep with her hair wet but by this time she didn't really care. All she wanted to just stop thinking for a while.

She collapsed into bed, heedless of the blue fur everywhere. Despite her exhaustion, sleep was slow in coming. Her mind whirled around and around itself until she finally slipped into a fitful slumber.

Chapter 17

June didn't understand why Walter wasn't at breakfast, but he was glad. After the night before, when he'd tried to hurt Maggie, he would be upset if the man had shown. Fortunately, there was no sign of him. This let him focus on eating and he devoured the sliced ham and scrambled eggs eagerly.

No one else was eating much. After his second helping he paused and looked around. Evan was smiling at him sadly, while Renee just looked into his plate and picked at his food. Diane and Gerald were nowhere to be seen.

"Okay?" he asked. He felt like he should be sad too and he frowned, staring at everyone's full plates. "Is bad?"

"Go ahead and eat," Evan told him with forced cheer. "Eat as much as you want."

June frowned and turned back to his food. He suddenly wasn't that hungry anymore. "No eat," he said after a minute. He picked up his plate and took care of it just the way Maggie showed him.

Renee followed him as he left the mess hall and headed for the infirmary. Before they could get there, the other grabbed his arm. "No, June," he said softly. "We can't go there."

"Maggie," June insisted. Maggie had seemed sad this morning, just like everyone else on the ship. She hadn't shown up for breakfast either. He was worried about her now. What if Walter really had hurt her?

"She's fine," Renee assured him. "She's just sleeping."

"See Maggie," June insisted stubbornly. He could feel his tail flicking back and forth across the floor with his agitation. His stomach was heavy with something he couldn't identify. It was dark and made him want to just run away from Renee and find Maggie.

Renee sighed. "Okay, you can see her."

June was forced to close his eyes before Renee would let him through. He heard Gerald talking to someone but couldn't hear enough words. There were a few heavy thuds that sent the fur on his tail straight up. He clutched to Renee's jacket and waited until they were past the infirmary. As they passed, June smelled something familiar. It reminded him of his time in the dark, a sharp metallic scent, and he shuddered at the memory.

When they were at the gym Renee let him open his eyes again. June looked at the chairs with the warm light longingly, but after a moment he turned away. He had to see where Maggie was.

She wasn't in the showers. With Renee still at his heels, he headed to the cabins. He made to enter Risa's code but turned and scowled at Renee. "No see!" he said shortly. It wasn't something that he had been told, just a feeling he had. He didn't know anyone else's code, so he figured it was some sort of secret.

Renee obligingly turned away. June entered the code and wriggled through the door even before it opened fully. When he saw Maggie soundly asleep in his usual place, he breathed a sigh of relief.

"See? She's okay," Renee said. He put a hand on June's shoulder and pulled on it gently. "We should leave her alone to sleep."

June hesitated. Even asleep, Maggie looked upset. Normally a sound sleeper, she was now quite restless. Seeing her writhe in her sleep made June uneasy. He didn't like to see her upset.

He touched her hand and she jerked away, eyes flying open. She looked between June and Renee in confusion. "Are we there yet?" she asked sleepily. "It doesn't feel like it's been that long."

"It hasn't," Renee said. "June was worried about you."

Maggie leaned forward and rubbed June's head with a smile. "Was he? I'm sorry, I didn't want you to be worried. Just go play, okay? I need to get a few hours of sleep."

Despite Maggie's smile, he could see something in her face. There were tight lines around her eyes that shouldn't be there. Her smile was wobbling like it would fade away any second. Even the hand on his head was trembling.

June didn't want Maggie to be sad. He didn't know why she was upset. Was it because of Walter? That man wasn't anywhere around now, so there was no reason to be sad anymore. "Okay?" he asked, even though he wished he could say so much more.

He wanted to tell Maggie that there was nothing to be sad about. He wanted to say that everything was going to be fine. He just didn't have the means to put those emotions into words.

Maggie's smile stopped wobbling for a second. "I'm okay, don't worry," she said softly. "I just need some sleep."

Sleep was usually good, aside from that day when he'd slept and woke up in pain. June didn't think something like that would happen again. Maggie didn't have a glass of that stuff that tasted bitter.

Maggie needed to sleep, he knew, and with that he crawled into the bed with her. Both Renee and Maggie started to protest but he persisted. Maggie had to wriggle backwards until she hit the wall, but soon enough June was able to curl up next to her. He patted her head and smiled at her. "Okay," he said. "Sleep."

"You don't have to do this," Maggie said wryly, but she settled down next to him anyway. Her hands were no longer trembling when she wrapped her arms around him. It was warm, so much like those warm lights but so different at the same time. He buried his face in her arm and sighed contentedly. He felt Maggie stroke his hair before relaxing, presumably falling back into sleep.

The door closed, though June couldn't see it. He peeked out and saw that Renee was no longer in the room. Where he was going didn't interest June in the slightest, and so he turned back to Maggie. It wasn't very comfortable like this, not really, but he wouldn't budge. Maggie was sleeping soundly now.

He settled in to wait for her to wake up.

Chapter 18

"This is a mess," Gerald sighed as Evan and Gary carried Walter's wrapped body into the freezer. First he had to deal with an alien boy, and now he had to deal with a murder on board. Sometimes he thought he was getting too old for this.

Still, there were older captains on duty in the military. He would deal with this. First things first.

Though, he found himself wondering as his crew gathered around him, what really was first? His duty should have been to Walter. His ship's cook had been killed because of an alien. June, granted, hadn't struck the final blow, but he knew that anyone else would be blaming the boy just the same. Anyone else would have murdered June on the spot and explained things later.

June, however, had proven time and again to be nothing more than a boy. His mannerisms were a bit odd at times but for the most part he was only a child.

He was even more of a child than most toddlers. In this he sympathized with Diane – June was completely innocent. It wouldn't do to kill a child to satisfy the bloodlust of the rest of the human race.

It was Gary that broke the silence. "June's dead, isn't he? We can't defend him from this." The janitor looked uncharacteristically worried.

Evan scowled. "Of course we can! Walter was the idiot that attacked him. Risa was just defending June and herself. She even said she didn't mean to kill him."

"That won't matter," Renee said quietly. He tapped his fingers on the table in a slow rhythm. When attention was turned to him, he shook his head. "It doesn't matter what happened. A human is dead and an alien isn't. I've seen all the shows with this theme. June's going to have to die in order to satisfy the public that justice has been served."

Diane sighed. "He's right. That doesn't mean I'm going to give up. I'm going to make it a matter of public record what happened."

"And what if our superiors decide to put a lid on this?" Evan demanded. "You could be thrown in jail. Worse, they could assign you to the front lines. Punishment detail. I know a few people who had that happen. None of them came back."

Renee chewed his lip. "It'd be worth it." His voice was soft but it was resolute. "I just can't sit by and let June die."

Gerald wished he could claim these men and this woman as his. It wasn't like the movies, where a crew was a crew no matter what. Duty shifts varied from voyage to voyage and there was no guarantee that he'd get any of them back the next time he set out. Still, this was a crew to be proud of. Maybe, he thought wistfully, if he was lucky.

"No matter what happens," he put in, and as he said this he looked each of his crew in the eye, "you are not to lie. I don't care if you think doing so will protect June. If you lie, and then are found out, it will only damage what little hope he has. Tell the truth to the letter. There's nothing saying that you can't emphasize things a bit." With that, he smirked a little. "The same events can have wildly different interpretations based on who tells it, after all."

There were a few puzzled looks while his crew sorted out what he meant. As they did, though, their faces lit up. "So you're saying that we can talk about how June isn't a monster while we're talking about why Risa defended herself," Evan said.

"I'm saying nothing of the sort," Gerald refuted, though he did so with a wink. "Now, even though we are only a few hours from Earth, it doesn't mean we can neglect our duties. Return to your posts. Dismissed!"

There was a chorus of, "Yes, sir!"s, and his crew scattered to the winds.

Gary disobeyed orders. Rather than returning to his daily drudgery, he instead hurried to his cabin. He had to tell Isobel about what happened.

It took far too long to get her on the phone, and even longer to explain what happened. He got the story out, though, and when he was done Isobel looked suitably troubled. "I'm afraid your friend Renee is right," she said at length. "It will be nearly impossible to save June's life now. Our only hope is to make his situation public before he can be executed."

"Diane already said she would," Gary told her. "Aside from that, I don't know how."

"Perhaps Risa could be convinced to," Isobel mused. "She's the one with all of the data. Make it public, demand that June sees justice. It might not be enough to keep him alive indefinitely, but it will be long enough for us to get the suitable people into place."

"I don't want June to suffer," Gary said helplessly. He truly didn't. Just watching the boy over these past weeks made the idea of him hurting intolerable. He clenched his fists in frustration. "I wish there was more I could do."

"Don't expose yourself!" Isobel ordered him sharply. "We need you there to act as our eyes. Your crew is likely to be kept together until matters are settled. Since you did nothing wrong I don't doubt you'll be given the freedom to communicate. We need you to tell us what goes on so we can be prepared to act."

Gary sighed. His palms stung from where his nails were digging in but he ignored the pain. It was nothing compared to what June would feel if he couldn't be spirited off.

"You're right," he said. No matter how much he wanted to take up arms and defend June until his last breath he couldn't. June would be best served by his current task. He still had an inkling of an idea, and he asked, "Do you still have contacts in JAG?"

Risa awoke to purring in her ear and her doorbell ringing. For a brief moment, in the land between dreams and reality, she wondered when she adopted a cat. The purring was soothing and she could feel the tension in her muscles giving way to bone-melting relaxation.

Then she opened her eyes to find slitted blue ones staring straight at her and she remembered. June smiled at her, his ears lazily tilting back and forth while his tail curled up in the air over his head. He lifted his hand to pat her cheek. "Okay?" he asked.

Risa couldn't help her smile back. Despite dreams troubled by the previous night's events she felt well rested. "I'm fine," she said. "Did you stay with me the whole time?"

June pushed his torso upright with several audible pops. The relief was evident on his face as he stretched and what sounded like his entire spinal cord popped. Even his tail went limp. Risa couldn't help her chuckle.

"So you did. Thank you," she said sincerely. "I really appreciate it."

June crawled out of the bed and wandered to the door. While Risa tried to get the motivation to get up, her son opened the door to let in the one still pressing the bell. Gerald stepped in and smiled at June, then looked to Risa.

"How long until Earth?" she asked. She slid out of bed and stood at attention, but her captain waved her down. She relaxed into a sitting position on the bed instead.

"Two hours, give or take a few minutes," Gerald replied. "That should give you enough time to get your data and materials ready for transport. If you want to spend the rest of your time with June, I can put Evan and Gary at your disposal instead."

Risa shook her head. "I can still perform my duties, Captain. It shouldn't take me two hours to get everything ready."

"Very good, Dr. Magee. I'll leave you to it then." Gerald left her and June alone. While the boy rummaged through his clothes, Risa found that she couldn't get up the will to move.

Two hours, she thought. Two more hours for June to be blissfully unaware of the hardships to come. If only those hours could last forever. She wished she could do more than argue futilely for his life.

Then she scowled at herself. This wasn't a time to focus on the future, not with it so close. Rather, she decided while she at last stood and began to change, she had better make these two hours the happiest of his life.

She had her back turned to June while she dressed in her uniform. It might be the last time she wore it, she thought wistfully as she smoothed her cuffs and her rank insignia. Still, June was alive. A uniform was just a set of clothes.

Ten minutes of her one hundred and twenty passed before she knew it. She turned from her thoughts figuratively and literally, smiling at June and reaching for his hand. He took hers without hesitation and beamed up at her.

"Time to go," she said softly.

It didn't take her very long to pack up her research and the samples she'd collected from June. The samples secured in a refrigerated contained - check. Her research saved and saved and saved again, three different copies – one for her personal use, one for her superiors, and one to be entered into the record. After that, she did a check of the infirmary one last time.

All through the half an hour it took to do this June stayed by her side. Despite her attempt at cheer, it seemed her son still knew something was amiss. He attempted to help her in her packing, though when he opened the cabinet with the syringes he backed up with a hiss. He looked affronted by Risa's amused laugh and pouted.

"Don't worry," Risa assured him. "Everything's going to be all right."

June couldn't help his small smile around his pout. Risa finished up and set everything she'd be transporting right by the exit hatch. "Now," she said as she turned to June, "we have an hour and twenty minutes before... well, it doesn't matter what."

June frowned. He could tell she didn't want to say something, but he either didn't want to ask or couldn't. So, instead, he patted his stomach. "Eat?" he asked.

Risa smiled. "Of course. Let's see if there's anything we can make."

It turned out when they got to the mess hall there was a lot. Gary and Renee were busily cooking in the kitchen while Diane and Evan stared at them. Gerald was nowhere to be seen, presumably in his office doing captain-like things. Spread across the table was everything that could be imagined coming from a ship's kitchen – everything from sandwiches to apple pie.

"What's up?" she asked. June dashed to the table and began loading a plate with things.

"These guys decided to cook," Diane stated. "They didn't say why. Something about the freezer being occupied and food going bad."

"And we had a lot of food since we raided the *Moreau*," Evan added.

"We ate as much as we possibly could," Diane continued. "There's still a lot left so eat up!"

Risa suspected that it was more than the freezer being emptied to put Walter's body in it. All eyes in the room kept shifting to June, who started munching happily. Once Renee and Gary realized that they'd arrived, they too kept looking at June and smiling sadly.

It wouldn't do to spoil the mood. Risa pushed those thoughts away and smiled at her crewmates. "Of course." She turned to the kitchen. "Thank you, Gary and Renee!"

"Enjoy!" they said in unison.

Risa didn't feel like eating that much, but after her skimpy breakfast she knew she had to force something down. With that in mind, she chose a few of her favorites from the spread and tried to enjoy herself. It wasn't very often in the military that one could eat a feast like this.

Forty minutes passed while they ate. June wolfed down everything he could while Risa ate more slowly. Once she finished as much as she could, she cut the pie and put a generous slice in front of June.

"Can't forget dessert," she said cheerfully when June looked up at her. "It's sweet and good. You should try it."

She picked up the fork and carefully readied a small bite of pie. Morsel raised with her hand under it to catch stray crumbs, she waited until June obediently opened his mouth. With great care she fed him the pie. He smiled at her as he chewed.

"Is it good?" Risa asked.

He nodded, but then he frowned. It looked like he rolled the pie over his tongue a little bit. Then his frowned deepened and he swallowed.

"Bad," he said. He picked up the plate and offered it to Risa instead.

"He likes apples but not apple pie," Diane said fondly. "Strange kid."

Risa smiled at June in understanding and took the pie. June watched her until she started eating it before turning back to the rest of the feast. It was a normal pie, she thought while she ate. She could taste the apples in it, bright and fresh, but they were smothered in thick syrupy sweetness. Maybe it was that that June didn't like?

It didn't matter. She finished the slice and waited for June. Finally he pushed his plate away and sat back with a contented groan.

Diane looked at her watch – forty-five minutes until they arrived. "What will you do now?" she asked.

"Whatever he wants," Risa replied.

It turned out all June wanted to do was bake under the sun lamps while they digested. Risa settled into her lounge and June into his, though she linked their hands in the space between the seats. The catboy didn't seem to mind. He stretched out under the warm light and dozed.

Ten minutes before arriving, Risa roused him. These last minutes she spent with her arms wrapped around him. No matter what happened she wanted to remember him like this, she thought. She wanted to remember how his body fit against hers while they sat. She wanted to remember how his tail idly thumped against her leg. She especially wanted to commit the way his ears twitched to her memory.

Two minutes before they landed, which Gerald's booming voice warned over the intercom, she leaned her head down and whispered to him.

"No matter what happens," she said, "I don't want you to be scared. No matter what. Be strong, you promise?"

June looked up at her, his expression one of confusion.

A thud echoed throughout the ship – they were docked. Risa squeezed June tightly. "I love you," she whispered. "I love you with all my heart, my son. My June. I love you."

She couldn't say those three words enough.

"Love," June repeated, then smiled. "Love Maggie."

She couldn't stop the tears rolling down her cheeks after that. She waved away June's worried frown. "Time to go," she said, and she couldn't help the frustration and bitterness in her voice.

June followed her obediently as she stopped by her cabin to pick up her few personal items. She stared a moment at the picture on her nightstand – the first June – before packing it away at the bottom of her bag. With her bag slung over her shoulder, she headed for the exit hatch.

Everyone stood at attention against the walls. Risa did the same, tugging June's arm to bring him next to her. He stood without protest, though his ears were slightly down and his tail was restless.

"It'll be okay," she whispered. "Be still."

His tail didn't settle. Instead, he clutched her arm and buried his face there. The hatch opening made him jump a foot in the air.

Soldiers strode in – marines, like Evan and Diane. They took one look around and spotted June immediately. "Creature found," one of them said. "Detaining it."

"Hold on," Risa protested immediately. She stepped out of formation and pushed June behind her protectively. "There's no need for any detaining. He'll come willingly. I need to speak with my supervisor regarding his fate."

She was shoved out of the way and into the wall. Strong arms gripped her wrists tight while shackles were thrown on them. "Dr. Risa Magee, you're under arrest for murder," her captor intoned. "You have the right to remain-"

"I know my rights," she said impatiently. She struggled back from her intimate relation with the wall so she could see. Her eyes sought and found June. He was backing away from the marines who were advancing on him, his tail twice its previous width. "June!" she cried.

The boy looked at her in fright, then dodged many pairs of seeking arms. He ran to her side and clutched her jacket tightly. "Maggie," he sobbed.

She knelt down and rested her forehead against his – if only her arms were free! "It's going to be all right," she said fiercely. "No one's going to hurt you. Don't fight them."

A marine got his hands on June and dragged them apart. The catboy was roughly manhandled into a crouch, a band was cinched around his chest to immobilize his arms, and that was topped off by having his hands cuffed tightly behind his back. June screeched in pain when his tail was careless trodden on.

He thrashed against the hands holding him, tears falling freely everywhere. "Maggie!" he cried. "Maggie!"

His voice echoed throughout the ship as he was dragged away. Risa couldn't help her own tears and she started after him. A marine grasped the chain around her wrists and caught her up short. "Let me go!" she wailed. "I have to go after him! He's my son!"

She received several cold looks from the marines around her. Without another word, she was marched off the ship. Risa listened despairingly to June's distressed cries echo as she struggled to rejoin him. It was futile – the hands on her arms were firm.

Chapter 19

She didn't know where the rest of her crew ended up. All she knew was that she was marched through corridors she'd never seen before. The marines dropped her in a bare room with only a toilet, sink and bed. After she was uncuffed she was left alone with only her thoughts.

Those thoughts were focused on only one thing: June. How was he? Had he been hurt? Killed? She paced around the room restlessly as those thoughts swirled around her head. Without a clock, she had no way to judge time. It seemed like forever passed before she finally got fed up with being ignored.

She walked over to the door and pounded on it. "Where's June?" she demanded loudly. "I need to see him. You can't keep me from him!"

No response. She pressed her ear against the thick metal of the door and listened. She couldn't hear any footsteps. There were no vibrations to tell of something moving outside the door. She knew that they had to be watching her somehow. They could hear every word she said.

"I have rights!" she shouted, smashing her fist against the door. "I demand to speak with someone! Tell me what you're going to do with my son!"

Still no answer. She shook out her throbbing fist and glared at the corners of the room near the ceiling. That's where cameras usually were, right?

She flopped on the bed with a frustrated sigh. Feeling powerless was not something she enjoyed. It wouldn't be so bad if she could just know what was happening to June. As much as she wanted to be optimistic, she could imagine what he was going through right now. The few aliens that made it to earth were always a bloodied mess by the time they got onto the news. When their inevitable executions came about, death was a mercy.

Imagining June in pain hurt. She tried to cast out the images she was conjuring but it was no use. Black eyes and lost teeth were the kindest pictures she could see. The reality was darker – slashed skin, broken bones. She couldn't help the frustrated and pained tears that leaked from her eyes at just the thought.

The door finally opened. Risa looked up and saw a strange woman walk in. "Who are you?" she asked, taking in the lack of a military uniform. The woman was dressed in a smart blue suit, a briefcase in her hand.

"I'm Isobel Barclay. Since no JAG lawyers want to handle your case I've been permitted to act as your counsel – pro bono, of course." She walked to the bed and sat next to Risa, settled her briefcase in her lap, and popped the latches open. "Thanks to your Captain's report we know all of the basic details of the events that happened last night aboard the *Descent*. Your admission is on record – you confessed to the crime in full witness to the rest of the crew."

"There wasn't a crime," Risa argued. Though she knew that it was going to happen this way she was still indignant. "I mean, yeah, Walter ended up dead, but it's his own fault. He tried to kill June, and when I got in his way he tried to kill me too. I was just defending myself."

Talking about it made it real and she couldn't help the sick feeling in her heart. She stared down at her hands again. When she looked at them, she could still see the red dots that had been there.

"And that," Isobel said with a nod, "is how we'll frame your case. Nevermind that Walter was attempting to eliminate an alien threat. Human life is the highest priority. Once you interfered, he should not have turned his blade on you. In that event it became a matter of self-defense."

"June isn't an alien threat," Risa argued. "I won't let you sacrifice him to save me. If me losing this case will help save him, I'll go to the judge right now and confess."

"You want to try to defend the alien boy?" Isobel asked. She shuffled through some papers and peered at one. "There is precedent, but to my knowledge the alien in that case lost and was executed."

"June's not an alien," Risa said with conviction. "He's just a little boy whose father warped his body against his will. He can't help what he was made into. Besides, cats are native to earth too, right? So he's technically not even an alien at all."

If Risa had known Isobel better she would have caught the faint smile on the other woman's face. Instead, all she saw was grim approval. "That's an interesting argument. I shall look into the legalities for how best to phrase that. So, just so I can present your plea to the judge, you're pleading not guilty by reason of self-defense?"

Risa nodded. "Please, see if you can arrange for me to see June," she begged. "I don't want him to think I abandoned him. I want to comfort him and tell him he doesn't have to be scared."

"So you really consider him your son?" Isobel asked. "When I interviewed your crew members they all emphasized that. They told me that you care about him a great deal and made sure to tell me that June isn't dangerous."

"I know he's not my blood," Risa explained. "But neither are kids that are adopted, right? I can't help but love him. He's so sweet and innocent. I want to protect him from everyone that wants to kill him for something that he can't help."

"The prosecution is going to argue that your judgment is compromised," Isobel warned. She pulled a picture out of her briefcase to illustrate her point. "According to them, June is nothing more than a surrogate for the son you lost. When you saw this boy you saw nothing more than your son reborn. It doesn't help that, if what Major Ledger says is true, June is what you were going to name your unborn son."

"That's not it at all!" Risa protested. In hindsight she could see how people could come to that conclusion. "I decided to take him in and he needed a name. June was the only one I could think of – I panicked, really. I looked over at my nightstand and saw that picture and I figured, my son wasn't going to need that name as much as this boy did."

"I can work with that. I shall also see about getting you in to see June. According to the judge, he won't be executed until after your trial." Isobel gathered her papers and shut her briefcase. "This will be your cell until your first hearing. The military is going to be quick to settle this so they can execute June. You should be in front of the judge by tomorrow."

Risa watched her lawyer go with mixed feelings. On the one hand she wanted to hope. She wanted to believe that this mysterious woman had good intentions. Yet there was just something odd about her. It was hard to believe that anyone would willingly help her defend June – a boy who wasn't an alien, but who certainly wasn't human.

She sighed and stretched out on the bed. There was nothing for her to do except wait.

Isobel closed her book with a sigh. Much as she wanted to be optimistic, she couldn't help but feel that this was all going to be in vain. The government was quite interested in keeping the status quo. If that meant letting an innocent boy like June get sentenced to die, well, they'd done worse things for the public good.

That didn't mean she was going to give up. She'd agreed to defend Risa and she would to the best of her ability. She just didn't think that she could defend Risa and keep June alive at the same time.

She glanced at the clock. Looking through the same books wasn't going to change what was in them. She stacked the books neatly, sticky notes poking out of them like a stout palm tree, and turned to her next task.

June's life couldn't be saved, not through the legal system. His only hope was if he could be removed from that system. If he could be taken from military custody, then he could be squirreled away with other alien refugees. He could live out his life free of worry.

With that in mind she picked up the phone, made sure the usual security protocols were in place, and dialed a number only she knew. She let it ring twice, hung up, waited a minute, then dialed again. It was picked up on the first ring.

"It's good to hear from you," her contact said from the other side of the line. There were never any names exchanged, just in case. Nothing was ever truly secure.

"Yes, it is. I don't have much faith in being able to save our target. How are things on your end?"

"We are setting events into motion that should see our target acquired. However, it might take longer than the timetable you gave us."

Isobel tapped her fingers on the table as she thought. "There are several tactics I can use to stall a judgment. Do not worry."

"Then we shall let you get to it. Goodnight."

Isobel set the phone down and planned her next move

Chapter 20

True to her lawyer's word, Risa found herself in a courtroom the next day. Unlike civilian court there was no jury, only a judge and a few generals from way up in the chain of command. Their uniforms positively dazzled in the stark lighting, the commendations and medals bright against their black backdrop.

There were a few people as witness, however. Unranked members of the military were in the seating area reserved for audience use. Even a few civilians, likely family members of military persons, were in attendance.

Risa looked at all of them as she marched into the room. She had been given time to clean up and a dress uniform to change into. The short skirt and closely tailored jacket were a deep navy to contrast the black of deep space, but their style was clearly that of the military's space division. Her pumps clicked smartly against the floor as she walked. She refused to walk slow or falter.

She would show no sign of doubt, she told herself with determination. What she had done had been unavoidable. It had been her life or Walter's. In that, she was confident in her choice. She was still sickened by it, but there was no time for that in the military. She had to look ahead at her goal: freedom for June. If she could walk free too, that was only a bonus.

Isobel awaited her at the defense table. "Our strategy is simple," the lawyer said after their brief greeting and they were seated. "Present June as a human, not as an alien. Show him to the judge how you saw him, not how he is. Emphasize his humanity, not his cat features, and use that as a justification for opposing Walter. They'll bring up your unborn son, we'll refute that the same way you said last night. Once we establish that June deserves protecting, your actions will be excusable instantly."

Risa nodded – it was as good a plan as she could come up with. "And what if they insist that protecting June doesn't excuse Walter's death?" she asked.

"Then we emphasize that your life was in danger rather than June's. Doing so will take the focus off of him, so it will be less likely that he will be spared. It's only a last resort." Isobel slid some documents at Risa so the doctor could look at them. "The prosecution is going to call these people as witnesses. On your behalf I'll be calling your crewmates. Is there anyone else you can think of that can help your case?"

Risa surveyed the list. Her crewmates were on there, but she doubted they'd give the testimony the prosecution wanted. The only names she didn't know had PhDs after them. "I can't think of any."

Isobel nodded. "It's looking like our case is going to rest on getting sympathy." She shot a glance at the shiny generals glaring down at them. "I'm not holding out much hope," she confessed.

"I don't care if I go to jail, just as long as I can keep June alive," Risa said with determination. She'd give up anything to save his life. If she was told that June would live if she ended her life right then, her only reaction would be to ask for a gun.

Well, after she got it in writing that June would live. A binding, notarized contract. It would be silly to kill herself on only a maybe. When it came to June, though, the fear of death was a distant partner to her desire to see him safe.

Shortly after their planning, such as it was, the trial was officially called to start. Risa couldn't really follow the legalities, but Isobel carried herself proudly and spoke well. The PhDs were called to testify first. They were, Risa found, psychologists who were very quick to call Risa a species traitor. They spouted medical jargon that sounded important to those without medical training. All Risa heard was, "Blah blah blah mental imbalance blah blah temporary insanity blah blah surrogacy."

All she could do was shake her head.

By the time the psychiatrists stopped talking long enough to let Isobel boldly challenge their views, medical textbook in hand, the judge called the trial to a halt for a night.

"Before we recess," Isobel said, standing to call attention to herself, "I'd like to discuss the issue of my client's bail. It is my request that she be released on her own recognizance."

"You want her free to murder someone else?" the prosecution scoffed.

Isobel glared coolly at the man. It was a look that was full of banked heat and the promise of dire things to come. After a moment, he coughed and looked away uncomfortably.

"I agree with the prosecution," the judge rumbled. "Dr. Magee is a danger to humanity. However, so long as she does not seek contact with the alien boy, I see no reason for her to not be released. She is confined to this base and is imposed a curfew of 1900 hours, a curfew that will be enforced by monitoring equipment."

Risa stood. She tried to ignore the bitter taste being barred from seeing June put in her mouth. Like she'd told Isobel the day previous, she wanted nothing more than to comfort him. He was probably terrified and no one would bother to try to explain anything to him. He was just an alien to these people.

If she disobeyed and tried to see him anyway, she told herself, it would only end badly for both of them. It would cement in the minds of her peers that she was a madwoman, and it would make them even more determined that June would die. If she persisted she didn't doubt that one of those in charge of watching him would decide to orchestrate an 'accident'.

In this case, she lamented, it was better for him to not try to see him. It didn't stop her heart from hurting.

"I accept those terms," she said humbly.

The gavel thudded. "Then we are in recess until tomorrow at 0900," the judge declared.

"Your belongings were delivered to your barracks," Isobel told her. "Now if you'll excuse me, I'm going to go try to get that one condition revoked. We can't convince everyone June's not a threat if you can't interact with him."

Risa nodded. "Please do. Even aside from that, I just want to make sure that he's okay."

While Isobel hurried after the judge, Risa turned to the military police. They secured a GPS tracker to her wrist and released her into the world. Twirling her new adornment around, Risa tried to think of what to do. The GPS device also had a handy clock display, presumably so she couldn't use ignorance of the time to break her curfew, and it was only an hour until then.

She sighed. It had been a long couple of days. It would be best for her to rest and regroup for the next day.

As she sat in the defense chair the next day listening to more of the same, she wondered if pleading guilty would be worth it. Listening to her judgment

[201]

being called into question over and over again made her blood boil. If she lost her temper, though, the prosecution would use that against her.

Finally, her crew was called to testify. Their testimony was overwhelmingly supportive. With every sentence they refuted every negative thing that had been said about her. When they tried to speak about June, though, the prosecutor shut them up quickly.

When Isobel was doing the questioning, it was all about June. They talked about their initial hesitation to accept him, then how he slowly changed their minds. Most of all, their testimony was overwhelmingly supportive of Risa's actions.

Once Evan left the witness box with a smile directed at Risa, the judge looked at his notes. "The prosecution has rested, Ms. Barclay. Do you have any witnesses to call?"

Isobel stood. "Yes, Your Honor. I'd like to call June to testify."

"Objection!" the prosecutor shouted. "The alien boy cannot talk so how is he to testify?"

"I just want you, the judge, to actually meet the boy my client killed to protect," Isobel explained quickly. "It will go far in establishing my client's state of mind."

There was a quick consultation between the judge and the generals. "I shall allow June to be brought to the court room," the judge said reluctantly.

They recessed for an hour while the arrangements could be made. Risa was restless as she waited. She paced back and forth, so many thoughts swirling through her head. She couldn't wait to see June again and see if he was okay. At the same time, there was a part of her that worried. Was he hurt? How had he been treated? Had he been fed these past few days?

Isobel spoke to someone in the audience while they waited. Risa didn't pay much attention to that – her lawyer had a life of her own, after all. She couldn't expect every moment of every day to be spent with her. So she waited, and paced, and fretted.

Finally, the doors opened and two marines strode in with June held tightly between them. Risa's heart rose, then sank almost instantly. June was limp, his tail dragging against the ground while he was carried. His eyes were open, at least, but they were half-closed and stayed focused on the ground ahead of him. The bruises Risa had feared were present, stark and purple against his skin.

Overall, it looked as if he'd given up.

"June!" Risa cried. The boy's ear twitched and he raised his head. When his eyes locked on Risa's, they shot wide open in shock.

"Maggie?" June asked, disbelieving. He twisted in the marines' grip violently and without warning. They were unprepared for it and dropped him to the ground. June landed on his feet and dashed as well as he could with his arms bound to his chest and his wrists cuffed in front of him.

Risa met him halfway and wrapped him up in the tightest hug she dared. He winced when her arms brushed his chest – more bruises or cracked ribs, it was impossible to tell. Despite his obvious pain, he gripped her jacket in his hands and buried his face in her chest.

"I'm sorry," she whispered, tears dripping into his blue hair. "I'm so sorry, June. Were you scared?"

"Scared," June repeated. He didn't have a chance to think it over because the marines were there, wrenching him violently away. Risa clutched his hands until they were ripped out of her own and watched, despairing, as her struggling son was planted on the witness stand. His cuffs were secured to a bolt that seemed made for this purpose. Even tied down, he kept struggling.

"Order!" the judge shouted. "Everyone settle down! Now that your witness is here, Isobel, please proceed with your questions."

Isobel returned from her conversation to Risa's side. "My apologies, Your Honor. I was distracted." She opened her briefcase and pulled out an apple. Under the watchful eye of the courtroom, she sliced the fruit, put it on a plate, and walked up to the witness stand.

June stopped struggling when she neared. "Apple," he said skeptically.

Isobel smiled. "Yes, June. You like them, right?"

"Apple taste good," June agreed.

Isobel picked up a slice and offered it to June. He lifted his hands but couldn't raise them far enough to take the apple. Instead, he leaned forward cautiously and gently lifted the bite from her fingers with his mouth. It only took him a second to wolf down the morsel.

"Now, Your Honor," Isobel said, her voice lightly admonishing, "does this look like the sort of beast we're all brought up to fear? When he fought free, I didn't see him go on a murdering rampage. He ran straight to Risa – the woman he views as his mother, and who cares for him as a son."

"This isn't questioning a witness," the prosecution argued.

Isobel nodded. "You're quite right. However, it would have been a disservice to introduce a living being as evidence. With your discretion, Your Honor, I would like to allow Risa and June to interact for a bit longer. That interaction is what I will enter as evidence. I will show that Risa, and June, are nothing more than a mother and son who were the target of a man who was blinded by his hate. In doing so I will show that Risa was well within her right to defend her son from harm. The victim's death was an unintended byproduct of her defending herself and her son."

"I object," the prosecution declared. "The alien boy was brought here under false pretenses."

"The last I heard," Isobel stated calmly, "both humans and cats are native to earth." She lifted a stack of documents from her briefcase. Risa recognized them as her very own research. "Genetic testing shows that June has cat DNA spliced into his own. Not some dangerous cat, but a common variety of housecat. If we are to argue semantics, I hereby submit that June is not an alien. He is not entirely human, that I will not deny, but neither is he not native to Earth."

For the first time both judge and generals looked impressed. "Overruled," the judge said at last. "Do as you will, Ms. Barclay."

June was freed, the boy rubbing his arms to get feeling back into them. Risa didn't hesitate to go to the witness stand and again embrace him. She was gentle this time, mindful of the wince from before. He clung to her with far less care.

"Maggie," the boy sighed happily. Risa could feel him relax in her arms and stroked his hair. "Scared," he repeated, too low for anyone else to hear.

"It's going to be all right," Risa promised. She felt the heavy stare of every person in the room on them and wondered what to do next. This was her chance to show that June wasn't a threat. Now how did she go about it?

"Dr. Magee," Isobel called, and Risa turned to see that her lawyer had sheets of paper and brightly colored markers in her hand. Instantly understanding Isobel's intent, she led June over and accepted the items.

"Sit," Risa told June gently. She sat right there on the floor and waited for her son to follow suit, which he did with a few winces. He watched intently as Risa picked up a sheet of paper, uncapped a marker, and started doodling.

She wasn't the best artist in the world. Her quick sketch of June was nothing more than a stickman with crude triangles for ears and a squiggly line for a tail. When she finished, she lifted the paper and beamed at June. "This is you," she told him gently.

June took the paper and frowned at it. His pains seemed forgotten while he scrutinized the bright colors. Risa uncapped another marker and pressed it into his hand. When he looked, she put the drawing down and gently nudged his hand down until the marker was pressed against the paper. The boy stared at the growing ink stain in confusion. When Risa lifted her hand away, he drew a few hesitant lines.

His face lit up when he saw what the marker could do. He thrust the marker back into Risa's hand and dove for a handful of the brighter colors. Risa sat back and watched him draw things with a contented smile on her face. His laugh of delight as he finished a drawing that scowled and looked suspiciously like Gerald echoed throughout the silent courtroom.

Several more drawings were created before the prosecutor stood. June looked up at him fearfully and shrunk into Risa. "Your Honor, how much more of this shall we have to endure? I believe the defense has had a chance to make her point."

"I agree. Just what were we supposed to gain from this?" the judge asked Isobel. Despite his words he was looking pensive now and his eyes didn't wander too far from June.

Isobel picked up a picture – Risa's stick June, with a carefully drawn companion courtesy of June. With the ponytail and white coat it was evidently meant to be Risa. "Permission to approach the bench," she requested. When the judge nodded she took the picture and laid it in front of him. "Just look at this, Your Honor. June is just a boy. Dr. Magee was well within her rights to protect him from Walter."

Whispering started up around the courtroom at those words. Risa held June close and waited for the judge's reaction. He picked up the picture and scrutinized it carefully.

"Noted, Ms. Barclay. Do you have any other evidence to present before we adjourn to await my ruling?"

Isobel shook her head. This was it, Risa thought. Her arms tightened around June. It was time to see what his fate would be.

Hope and doubt warred within her. She wanted to be optimistic, but there were never happy endings for the inhuman. There were just so many whispers around her and not all of them seemed negative. The judge's expression was hard to read as he nodded. "Very well. We are adjourned. I will issue my ruling in three days."

It would take that long, Risa mused, because it was Friday. So, Monday it was. Three more days for certain that June would still live. After that… well. Risa wouldn't think about that because if she did she wouldn't be able to let June go.

June was bound up as tightly as before and dragged out. Risa tried to chase after him but was barred by court officers. "The order preventing you from seeing him is still in place," one of them grumped at her. Then he smirked nastily. "This is the last time you'll ever see him," he said forebodingly.

Risa glared at him. "And this might be the last moment you're ever able to father children," she warned. The officer looked visibly disturbed and backed down. Risa walked past him and out of the courtroom.

She blinked in surprise at all of the cameras that were pointed firmly her way. Reporters that had been busily chatting away amongst themselves caught sight of her and pounced. She was quickly overwhelmed by the barrage of questions directed at her.

Chapter 21

Major General Trevor Braxton shut off his TV in distaste. "I can't believe this," he muttered under his breath as he stared at the blank box. "How did it even happen?"

He sighed and rubbed at his aching forehead. "I'm too old for this." Hadn't it already been decided that aliens were bad? Why was it even an issue?

Only a toddler when aliens had first made their presence known, he nonetheless remembered his encounter with them. It was too dreadful to even recall their faces – their blank faces, white eyes staring straight into his soul…

He shuddered, again ruthlessly repressing that memory. Everyone else had died. Now, fifty years later, his hair's whiteness was hidden with deep black dye. He kept it so short that his scalp was quite visible. It wasn't that he was going bald, he deluded himself. His hair was just too short and he'd let it grow out soon.

His dark brown eyes were troubled as he rolled the day's events in his head. Things had been going so smoothly. The alien boy was well on his way to the execution chambers. Risa would be found guilty of murdering another human to protect alien scum. And sanity would once again be restored to his forces.

Braxton glowered. It was all a civilian's fault. No one knew who, or why, but the culprit would be found soon enough. A camera – something that had been barred from the courtroom – had found its way into the closed proceedings. A live feed ensured that the entire world saw the alien boy. Now there were cries from all over the world clamoring for his life to be spared. He didn't doubt that by dawn he'd get those orders.

He glared at the papers on his desk before his eyes fell on a stack. He picked them up and looked through them, his frown gradually turning into a smirk. Maybe things weren't a total loss after all.

June dragged his feet as he was dragged by his bound wrists into a blindingly pristine room. The person dragging him didn't even look at him, and he was tripped up by his own tail several times. Each time, his tail screamed at him in pain – he was sure some of his fur was scattered in the hallway behind him.

He hated this. He wanted Maggie. Ever since the room with a lot of people, what Maggie had called a court room, he hadn't seen her. When he asked for her, he was ignored. When he cried and begged to see her, he was scoffed at. No one around him seemed to care about him. A few, after he'd begged a moment too long, even struck out at him.

The bruises all over his body throbbed when he was jerked forward a bit too hard one last time. He stumbled, but the firm grip around his wrists prevented him from falling to his knees. Another hand grabbed him and pulled him forward. June dared to look up to see that another person had taken hold of him. His tormentor turned and finally spared him a look. It was a dark one, filled with hate and triumph, one that filled June with fear.

The new person pulled on his hands again. It was a gentle tug, but when June looked at her he knew he couldn't resist it. Her face was hard and cold, just like the man who had brought him into this room.

June stared at her. She was dressed just like Maggie, in the black pants and shirt and white jacket. She was several inches taller than Maggie, though, and she towered over June. Her hair was light-colored and cropped close to her head. Her pale blue eyes were frigid behind the bangs that partially obscured them from view.

June didn't want to follow her. He glanced the way he'd come, but more people like Evan and Diane now blocked the way. They lifted their weapons with gleeful expressions as if daring him to attempt escape.

There was nowhere to go. All June could do was follow the gentle pull on his wrists until he was next to a bed. It was so very similar to the same bed in

Maggie's office, but it felt just as pristine and cold as the rest of this room.

"Sit down," the woman ordered. June did as he was told and wished there was something else he could do. He had a bad feeling about this. That feeling intensified when he looked around and saw equipment he recognized. Everything surrounding him had also been in Darryl's lab.

He knew his ears were back, but he couldn't help it. He remembered how each and every object had been used on him. He remembered the pain and discomfort, how Darryl had only looked on impassively while he screamed.

A shudder of revulsion ran through his body. "Scared," he whispered. He hoped he had the right word. This was one of the ones Maggie had whispered to him at their brief reunion.

The woman paused and frowned. "What did you say?" she demanded.

"Scared," June repeated, louder. His tail twitched upwards within reach and he grasped it in one bound hand. He felt his heartbeat quicken and he couldn't help his fearful shiver. Tears were gathering in his eyes, but he suppressed the instinct to hiss. Doing that only made the humans around him frightened. They hurt him when they were frightened.

The woman hesitated, then released his wrists. He dropped them to his knees gratefully. They throbbed with every heartbeat and resting them helped ease the pain. He tensed when she reached to his head, but all she did was brush hair flat soothingly. "I can't promise everything will be fine," she said softly. June understood only a few words, but the gentle voice was soothing. It was like Maggie.

He ducked his head. "Scared," he insisted. He wanted to go back to Maggie. He wanted to be back on the ship with everyone who smiled at him. No one on the ship hurt him. If only he could be back there – his wrists wouldn't hurt, his body wouldn't ache.

The woman stroked his head a few times more. Then she grabbed his wrists again in a gentle grip. "Lie down," she ordered.

June nodded and did as he was told. The woman kept his wrists elevated until he was flat on the bed. One of the guards by the door came over and pressed a device to the metal around his wrists. It fell away.

Before June could act on his newfound freedom, it was again taken away. The woman and the guard each took a wrist and pressed it into a cradle on the bed. The woman's actions were gentle – his wrist was lowered gently into the cradle. The guard, however, slammed his wrist down. Pain shot up his arm and June whimpered.

The woman glared at the guard even as she pressed a button. Metal shot up from the cradles and June found that he was shackled to the bed. His captors let go of his wrists – there was no longer a need for them to be held. His ankles were maneuvered into two more cradles, and another button press saw them restrained as well.

The guard frowned at the tail thumping agitatedly between June's legs. He rummaged in a drawer and came up with something silver. He tore off several strips of the silvery material. His grip on June's tail was firm and unmerciful while he applied the silver strips. Once he was done, June found that his tail was tied down as well.

The tears June was trying to hold back finally fell free. He was helpless. He struggled against his bonds, but he could hardly even squirm. Even the tip of his tail couldn't wriggle. He looked up at the woman. She wasn't trying to free him, but she was gentle. Maybe, just maybe, she would be kind and release him.

There was no luck to be had on that front. The woman picked up several tools and brought them to June's bedside. One of them was a needle and he tensed at the sight of it. There was no soothing voice to assure him it would be okay. He twisted in his bonds but there was no escaping the prick in his elbow. His blood flowed onto a cloth the woman had on his arm.

The woman was efficient. Only a minute later there was a tube connected to his arm. The tube led to a bag full of clear liquid. June could feel the cool fluid flowing into his veins. It chilled his arm, which also blissfully numbed some of the worst bruises there.

"Scared," he sobbed. He wished he knew the words to try and make the woman free him. "Maggie," he moaned. Why couldn't she be here? If she was here, she would free him and take the needle from his arm.

She would soothe his hair and ears back, whisper soothing words in his ear.

The woman brushed a few tears from his cheek gently. When June looked up at her, her expression was regretful. "Please," June whispered. It was a word one of his abusers taught him. When he said it, they were merciful sometimes. Maybe this woman would be merciful too.

She turned her head away and took a deep breath. Her hands found another syringe and a bottle of clear liquid. More tears fell from June's eyes at the sight of them, but this needle went nowhere near his skin. The woman filled the syringe and found a small knob on the tube in June's arm.

She hesitated. Her hands trembled, and her eyes found June's again. The boy stared up at her, pleading, but she closed them and took a deep breath. On the exhale, her fingers pushed in the plunger.

June stared at the tube. He couldn't tell which was the liquid from the bag and which was from the syringe. A hand took his and gripped it tight. He squeezed back, then lifted his eyes to the woman's. Her other hand went to his head and stroked his hair gently. "Don't worry," she said softly. "You won't feel a thing."

His eyes grew heavy. His pounding heartbeat slowed. Breathing became an effort. He clutched the hand around his, fear gripping him. His attempts to draw breath were labored.

"Scared," he whimpered. Even that was weak.

"It's okay," the woman said softly. "Just sleep, June. Everything will be all right."

"Maggie," he managed. His voice was barely a breathy exhale. Darkness was closing in on the edges of his vision. No matter how hard he tried, he couldn't keep his eyes open.

The last thing he saw was the woman's face. Tears were streaming down her cheeks. Then the darkness overtook him.

Chapter 22

"We find you, Dr. Risa Magee, not guilty of murder by reason of self-defense," the judge declared that Monday morning. "However, you have been found guilty of ignoring military protocol. In light of your years of service you are to be honorably discharged from the armed forces."

Risa couldn't decide what she was thinking. Just so long as June was okay, she told herself fiercely. As long as he was okay she could endure any punishment. She stood tall.

"As far as the non-human boy June is concerned, it has come to our attention that there are ethical issues that need to be addressed. Until such time as they can be resolved, this court cannot in good conscience issue an order for his disposal." The judge was as impassive as ever, but the generals behind him were scowling. "He is to be held at the research facility so that he can be studied until such time that his fate is decided."

Tears dripped down Risa's face at this proclamation. He was safe! She couldn't hold her composure and covered her face with her hands. June was going to live. Decisions like this could take years. Until then, even as a lab rat, June was going to be safe.

"These proceedings are adjourned," the judge finished. Isobel patted Risa's back until the doctor's tears stopped falling.

"Your approach worked," the lawyer cheered her up. "June will live. Even as a civilian doctor your insight into him is invaluable. I don't doubt that they will allow you to see him again."

Risa nodded. "Of course," she said. "I'm just so glad."

"My work here is done, I suppose." Isobel produced a business card. "Anything involving June will be my pleasure to handle. No charge. He's a wonderful child."

"Thank you," Risa told her. There were no words that could convey the depth of her gratitude. All she could do was clutch the card and smile through her tears. "Thank you."

There were reporters waiting for her outside the courtroom. They asked the usual questions – was she satisfied with the verdict, would she be seeking her job back, etc. She said what they wanted to hear and escaped quickly enough. Her attention was focused on getting back to her barracks so she could pack up.

She wanted to go see June, it was true, but now it wasn't as pressing. He was going to live. Every moment with him was still precious, but no longer would they be few. She could turn her attention to matters that were equally demanding.

Now that she was no longer a member of the military she would have to find a place to stay near the base. She took the long road back to her barracks, eying the world outside the base. It was tall and metal, its shine scuffed by years of wear. Wheeled cars were still commonplace on the roads, but no longer did they burn fossil fuels. Only the very rich could afford private shuttles to soar above the cares of the common folks.

There were apartments nearby, she remembered. One of her former bunkmates had babbled on about them constantly before dying on the fringes of charted space. She wouldn't be booted off the base immediately. She could get into those apartments on her remaining wages and find a new job.

So. She had a plan. After she got to her barracks and began packing she would go see June. She would tell him the good news. Most of all, she would hold him in her arms. Enjoy the feeling of him being alive.

It was with that in mind that she arrived at her barracks. There were more reporters but she walked past them without stopping. She had things to do. When she got to her door, though, she found that Gerald was waiting for her.

"Captain," she greeted. "I didn't expect you here." She unlocked her door and waved him inside. "Come on in. It's been a while since I've been here so I apologize for the mess."

"There's something you need to know," Gerald said softly. "You should sit down."

She looked around at her room – her belongings from the ship were there, so she picked up that bag first to sort through. "I was found not guilty, Captain. Isn't that great? I can't wait to go see June again. He'll be excited too."

"Sit down, Risa. I can't order you anymore, but please." Gerald's expression was far from joyful. Risa's happy mood faded once she got a good look.

"What's wrong?" she demanded. A cold feeling settled in her gut. Had something happened?

It couldn't be June, she thought. Even as she did she knew that a judgment in his favor meant nothing to the extremists. They would still seek his death.

"Sit," Gerald coaxed. She did.

"He's okay," she whispered. "He has to be. The judge said he was going to be. They weren't going to kill him."

"There was a conflict in orders," Gerald told her gently. His kind voice was horrible because Risa knew what he was going to say. She knew and tears gathered in her eyes.

"There's a mistake," she insisted. "There has to be."

"I'm sorry. I saw the video with my own eyes. It happened during the proceedings this morning while everyone's attention was focused on you." Gerald pulled a memory drive out of his pocket and put it in Risa's limp hand. "The ones responsible will be disciplined, of course. No one knows where the orders came from but the ones who carried them out will be punished."

Risa clutched the small bit of plastic in her hand. It wasn't possible. June was supposed to be okay. Her chest felt empty. Her tears began to fall on the device. "It's not true," she insisted. "It can't be true!"

Gerald's hand on her shoulder was too heavy. His deep voice sounded like it was coming from a distance as it murmured, "I'm so sorry, Risa, but June's dead."